# 13 STEPS TO HELL

## *(The Gavel and the Gun Vol. 2)*

## JACK R. STANLEY

Wrightbridge Press

13 Steps To Hell

(The Gavel and the Gun Vol. # 2)

by

Jack R. Stanley

This is a work of fiction. Any resemblance to any persons, events or localities is purely coincidental and beyond the intent of the author and publisher.

jacks@wrightbridgepress.com
www.jackrstanley.com

*To Mary Lee who makes all things possible.*

# CHAPTER 1

Both whites and Indians despised half breeds in the The Nations. A growing number of white men took Indian wives in order to have access to otherwise off-limits Indian land. But the offspring of these unions were not welcomed or trusted by either heritage.

Eben Snee was half Cherokee and half German-American. He gave as much contempt as he received. As a breed, Snee grew up skinny, but rock hard of limb and merciless of spirit. Through his one green eye and one gray, he saw a world where he didn't fit in. He gathered other half whites around him, and they became known as troublemakers, hell raisers, and complete malcontents.

Snee loved to chase wild hogs through towns and Indian villages using the creatures for target practice. He carried a Navy Colt and was a dead shot. He delighted in wounding the feral pigs instead of killing them just to watch the animals suffer and struggle.

Snee shot and killed farmer Harmon Stilegebouer, a middle-aged farmer and his Osage wife, Thistle, miles from any town. The vicious half breed wanted nothing more than to steal their horse and take the few air-tights of beans on their farm shelf. The Stilegebouer farm was on the edge of the Arbuckle Mountain in the south-central part of the Territory.

After the crime, Snee used the dead couple's horse to move their bodies to a crevasse up in the mountains. There he dumped the pair assured that no one would ever find them.

Snee continued his outlaw ways and became known as a shootist and an evil young man. He loved to show off by tossing his revolver into the air, letting it spin end over end a couple of times before he caught it and nailed a preselected target.

But when Snee was drunk, he was a danger to himself and anyone near him. Deputy Marshal Cornelius Carney took Snee into custody in McAlester. Carney was a threatening figure. At six foot three and two-hundred-fifty-three pounds, the hard-edged, mustached, Deputy Marshal projected an air of no-nonsense. He handled prisoners none too gently. Quick with both his fists and his gun, Carney managed to arrest Snee and put the fear of God in the half breed. In an attempt to save himself from the Marshal's wrath, Snee blurted out a confession of the Stilegebouer murders with all the details. He even signed a document describing the murders.

It was only when Snee sobered up that he realized he had paved the road to his own hanging.

* * *

Cautious and trail-wise Light Horse Policeman, Spotted Antelope, had two warrants in his jacket. The Creek wore double braids of dark hair from under his round crowned hat. His deeply weathered skin testified to his twenty-six years as a lawman in The Nations. He levered a .44-70 cartridge into his Winchester before he called out to the shabby structure.

Spotted Antelope shouted, "Hello, the house. Clemente Bays, you are under arrest!"

Forty-year-old Bays had been living with two younger Indian women and had a still boiling away behind the barn. Bays stepped out of the house, pulling his suspenders up over his shoulders. He was a man of average height, which meant he was taller than the five-foot, eight-inch Policeman. Bays had a .44 pistol in his hand with his gunbelt around his waist.

"Who says, I'm under arrest?"

"Spotted Antelope, Light Horse Police," the Indian eased his rifle over to cover Bays.

"Looks like we have a kind of Mexican standoff here," Bays said, cocking his pistol and raising at the lawman.

"Are you ready to die?" Spotted Antelope said. "We can kill each other if that's what you want. It is a good day for dying."

Rather than answer the question, Bays asked, "What are the charges?"

"Bigamy and making whiskey."

"Bigamy? I ain't married t' anybody."

"You're living with two women and have been for several years. That's bigamy. And I can smell your still from here. Are either of these charges worth dying for?"

Bays scratched his stringy gray beard.

"You by yourself?" Bays asked after a moment.

"It doesn't matter. You are under arrest. If you resist, you're adding a whole year to any sentence if you live. You'll hang if you kill me."

After another thought, Bays lowered his pistol, uncocked it, and dropped it to the dirt. He let his gunbelt slip off his shoulder to the ground, too. He raised his hands.

* * *

Hence Blevin had survived the War Between The States and scavenged his way back to Texas only to be slaughtered in Choctaw country of the Oklahoma Indian Territory. At 21, he and his 16-year-old bride, Adell, had scraped together close to 300 head of wild, rangy cattle. The herd was all that remained of their combined family ranches. Taking a crew of four, they drove their meager heard up the Shawnee Trail. This path crossed the Red River above Dallas, cut northeast through The Nations towards the railhead at Sedalia, Missouri.

There were three cattle routes through the Oklahoma Indian Territory. Hence and Adell took the shortest path. The other two were the

Chisholm Trail, through the middle of the Territory, and the Great Western Trail to the west.

A group of Choctaw warriors led by War Dog, a fighter who knew only hate for the white man and what had happened to his tribe over the years, directed the raid on the cow camp. The band of nine body painted and screaming savages hit the camp at dawn. They murdered Adell before they realized she was a woman. Hence killed one of the attackers before he was wounded and captured. Three other sleeping riders were shot or lanced in their bedrolls.

War Club, sinewed and hard-muscled, hung bleeding Hence spread eagle two feet above the smoldering campfire face down. Slowly the wounded young man cooked to death.

When the warriors discovered Adell was a woman, they stripped her and used her body for their pleasure.

Only the nightrider, Ford Telton, 15, a former slave, escaped. He witnessed the barbaric attack and the pillorying of his boss before he raced away in total panic. An hour later, while resting and watering his exhausted mount by a creek in a gully, he saw the smoke on the horizon. It was a prairie fire the Indian's had set to cover their crime. The rushing blaze spooked Telton's horse, which jerked away from him in terror and fled in fear.

The young cowhand soaked himself in the water and hunkered down under the lip of the outcropping. The raging enferno swept over him. He had to gasp for air — but he survived. On foot, he made his way across the charred land in the direction of Arkansas.

# CHAPTER 2

The editors and publishers of Ft. Smith's two newspapers sat in the back of Judge Parker's courtroom. The Judge held court six days a week from eight-thirty in the morning until six in the evening. Claxton Landers represented the Ft. Smith Daily Ledger. The balding, wire-rimmed glasses-wearing journalist, scribbled on a note pad with a pencil. On the opposite side of the gallery sat squat Joseph (Pick) Pickering of The Vindicator. Pick had a chip on his shoulder and always looked for something negative to write about the "Yankee Judge." He always seemed to wear his green eye-shade. It was a running joke in town that he slept in it.

The goings-on in court were always good copy if not headline material. At the moment, a ratty overall-wearing man of either forty or ninety, it was difficult to tell, was complaining about his arrest for making and selling liquor in the Indian Territory.

"A man's property is his and ain't no lawman got the right to come on it," Selmer Korns declared. "That's the law, ain't it?"

"Unless an officer has a lawful warrant to search and arrest," Judge Parker said. The thirty-six-year-old jurist had brown hair, a trimmed mustache, and goatee. Of average height, Parker was in no way physically threatening.

"Well, how's a lawman t' know what's on my property without violating my rights?"

"According to written testimony, you have been seen selling your elicit products in Reno City."

"Whoever said that is a damn liar."

The Judge rapped his gavel on his desk.

"There will be no foul language in this court!"

"'Damn' is in the Bible," Korns said, looking around.

"Have a seat, Mr. Korns. You have a good attorney, and you will get justice in this court."

"Hell, Judge, that's jest what I'm a' scare of."

The jury and those in the gallery burst into laughter as the Judge gaveled the court to order again.

* * *

The Sidewheeler was the best saloon in Ft. Smith. Ever since the owner and chief bartender Jules Morgan had been acquitted of attempted vigilante murder, he was a changed man. The slightly overweight, sandy-haired forty-one-year-old, had indeed been guilty of the crime. However, all the evidence was circumstantial, and the man the vigilantes were trying to hang, one-legged Confederate vet, Stony Welch, had been saved before he could be lynched. It was also true that before Judge Parker arrived, the local citizens depended on vigilante justice because there was no other.

Jules had offered part ownership in his business to his attorney, Temple Houston. Houston, the son of the famous Texas statesman Sam Houston, always dressed in white, whether he was in court, in his law office, or gambling at the Sidewheeler. The slender and handsome lawyer/gambler/gunfighter had shoulder-length blond hair, thin mustache, and stood almost six feet.

The new bar in The Sidewheeler came from New Orleans and was beautiful mahogany. The saloon now had the air of an exclusive gentlemen's club. New light fixtures and tables all contributed to the upgrade. The rougher elements tended to take one look once inside and decided to favor one of the less refined drinking establishments.

Kerwood Wannamaker stepped inside and found the place comfortable. But he was on a mission and didn't even approach the bar. He located the attorney he was looking for at a table playing cards with four other men.

Wannamaker was a successful rancher and dressed like it. At fifty-two, he was still vital and fit. Wannamaker wore a string tie on his starched white shirt. He was dressed in a black suit and matching Stetson. His tanned face was not as weathered as many men his age, but the crow's feet at his eyes testified to his age. He had a prominent nose and bloodshot brown eyes.

Stepping up to the table where the game was in progress, Wannamaker said, "Mr. Temple Houston?"

The attorney remained focused on the cards in his hand. "I'll raise you twenty," He said and tossed four blue chips into the collection at the center of the table. Two players folded their cards and sat back. A salesman in a bowler hat matched the lawyer's bid and called. The salesman spread his cards on the table. He had three kings, a seven, and a duce. Houston showed his cards, four trays, and a queen.

The salesman sagged as the remaining player, another gambler, made a frustrated face and threw in his cards. Houston raked in the chips as he looked up at the rancher.

"At your service," Houston said.

"I'd like to hire you to represent me," Wannamaker said.

The lawyer removed his white hat and swept the chips in front of him off the table and into his hat. He stood and asked, "And you are?"

"Kerwood Wannamaker," the rancher said, extending his hand. Temple took the proffered hand and shook it.

"Let us retire to another table."

Wannamaker agreed. Together they moved to a table near the colored glass window, and Houston took a seat with his back against the wall.

"A beer?" Temple asked.

The rancher sighed and nodded.

"Jules," Temple called "two beers if you please."

"Coming up," the co-owner/bartender called back.

"I believe I've heard of you, Mr. Wannamaker," Temple said. "You own a considerable spread East of Van Buren."

"That's me. And my son, Tyler. The Circle W."

"And what kind of legal service can I offer you?"

Jules arrived at the table with two beers. He parked the mugs in front of the men. Temple gave his hat to the bartender.

"Can you cash these in for me, Jules? I'll check with you later."

"Sure thing," Jules said and retreated with the hat full of chips.

When the two were alone again, Wannamaker said, "I'd like for you to represent me in court against a charge of murder."

"Whom did you kill?"

"My wife."

# CHAPTER 3

Mace Truax was the Marshal for Judge Issac Parker's court — the Western District of Arkansas. The thirty-two-year-old former Army Cavalary Major and Texas Ranger was back in Ft. Smith and trying to get a hand on his new position. The six-foot five-inch Marshal had spent his first two months on the job traveling across the Indian Territory with John Browneagle, a Choctaw Light Horse Policeman. Mace wanted to know what the role of his deputy marshals was like. A strong man with a deep voice and bright blue eyes, Mace had confronted the soulless, vicious killers and criminals who made the land of the Indian Nations their hideaway. He came to understand what the U.S. Deputy Marshals would have to face for their $500 a month.

Mace had gone to West Point and was a major when he resigned from the Army and arrived in Ft. Smith. He was looking for something to do with his life and experience. He had stepped in and stopped two drunk miners from killing each other in The Sidewheeler saloon. The next day he'd been asked if he would be interested in the open office of U.S. Marshal for the court of the Western District of Arkansas. Mace was offered the position by the newly arrived judge, Issac Parker. Mace's predecessor, Marshal Bart Zolan, had become a killer, and no

Deputy Marshal was willing to arrest the man. Mace made it his job to capture the man and him bring to justice. Zolan was sentenced to death and hung in Ft. Smith.

Judge Parker had told him that even second to his tasks managing the Marshal's office, his main duty was to recruit more deputies. The court was allowed two-hundred men to ride the seventy thousand square miles of what had become a haven of thieves, gun and whiskey runners, rapist and killers.

The new Marshal had taken a room for himself above Howell Keeling's Mercantile and had located a house for his widowed sister and her two daughters. Her husband, Benson Vickery, had been killed by a Sioux war party. Mace had taken care of his sister at his Army postings ever since her husband died. Now he had sent for Mena and the girls to come to Ft. Smith.

Naturally, there was a significant amount of paperwork required for the Marshal. But Mace was determined that one of his most important chores was to have a face-to-face with each Deputy Marshal now on the payroll whenever they came to town. Knowing who these men were and what their strengths were would help Mace in his recruiting assignment.

The very first on his list was Heck Thomas. The Georgia native had been the enlisted soldier in charge of Union General Philip Kearny's horse and equipment. The one-armed Union commander died at the Battle of Chantilly at Fairfax, Virginia. Confederate General Robert E. Lee wrote a letter to Kearny's widow, and Heck Thomas was then allowed to return the Union general's horse and equipment to the fallen officer's wife along with General Lee's letter.

For the past three years, Thomas had been a Deputy U.S. Marshal under Judge William Story. Before Story could be impeached, the corrupt judge resigned. The court he left was a mess. Only half the two-hundred authorized Deputy Marshals were ever hired. Many of those proved to be everything from ineffective to criminal. Heck Thomas was a prime exception.

The respected Deputy lived in a rooming house on North 5th Street. Mace walked over and knocked on the Deputy's door at eight

A.M. It was coming on toward fall, and there was a hint of cooling in the September air.

Thirty-four-year-old Thomas opened the door standing in his socks. Thomas wore a thick and heavy mustache down to the corners of his mouth. He was beginning to lose his brown hair, but his keen hazel eyes marked him as an intelligent man not to be fooled with. He wore only one pistol, a weathered hat, and a corduroy jacket, collarless shirt, and canvas trousers.

"Heck Thomas?" Mace asked.

"Marshal," the Deputy said. "Come in."

First, Mace offered his hand. Heck brought a cocked Peacemaker Colt .45 from behind his back and stuck it into his belt. He shook Mace's hand, firmly looking Marshal Truax in the eyes. Mace found the room neat. A Henry .44-.70 lay on a table against one wall near the window where it was being cleaned.

"What can I do for you?" Thomas asked.

"I wanted to meet the man who should have been in line for the badge I wear."

Heck Thomas smiled, and his eyes twinkled.

"Not at all, Marshal. If the job had been offered, I wouldn't have taken it."

"Why not? You're certainly qualified for it."

"True, but so are you, Marshal. If fact, you have more experience commanding men than I do."

"In the military — but you have the experience in law enforcement, I don't."

"I'm not an office man. I think the paperwork would defeat me the first week. No, I'm better out in the field. I'm pretty good at what I do - - and I like it. You are welcome to the Marshal's job. And call me, Heck."

"Then, I'm Mace to you, Heck." The two men nodded to each other. "I'm relieved to hear you're not sore about not being even asked if you wanted the job. From what I hear and from the reports I've read, you are excellent out in the Territory. What did you just bring in, eight — nine prisoners?"

"Nine. That's the job, isn't it?"

"It is."

"Have a seat, Marshal," Thomas said, picking up a copy of The National Police Gazette out of the one overstuffed chair.

"Thank you," Mace said, and he sat. Heck pulled over his chair from the table. "I'd like to pick your brain for what we need to do to help you do your job."

"Your allowing each deputy to draw $50 advance from the bank is a good beginning."

"How about the equipment? And where do I look for other deputies?"

"Most of us prefer our own gear. Standardizing it would be a bad decision. We're not military, and what we do we do best each of us do in our individual way. An allowance for equipment would be nice."

"I'll see what I can do. How about men to hire?

"My suggestion would be, first, to find respected lawmen who have proven the can handle themselves. Then I'd looked for a big ranch or trail drive Segundo."

The Segundo was the second in command on a ranch directly under the foreman. Or he was under the trail boss on a cattle drive. Such men handle any gun work situations might require.

"And, Marshal, I wouldn't overlook other ex-military like yourself. As long as a man is of good character and can handle himself, those are the ones you want."

"Thank you, Heck." Mace stood. "When do you expect to be back at it again?"

"Mr. Cross, the judge's assistant, said I could take a couple of weeks off. He also said when I come back, I should see you about new warrants."

"Enjoy your time off," Mace said. The two men shook hands again. "I'll see you when you're ready."

# CHAPTER 4

Mace Truax waited on the wharf as the sternwheeler, "The Arkansas Traveler," tied up. Beside the Marshal stood Delta Keeling Wadsworth. The deep chestnut-haired beauty was the daughter of Howell Keeling, owner of a local Mercantile and Mace's landlord. Mace met Delta shopping in her father's store and looking for a room to rent. Widowed a little over a year now, the twenty-six-year-old had a nice figure but still dressed in all black. She and Mace had gone to a barn dance together and had been keeping company ever since.

On the lower deck of the riverboat stood Mace's sister, Mena, twenty-nine, and her two daughters, six and four. The three all waved to Mace as soon as they spotted him on the dock.

When the gangplank was in place, Mena and her girls were the very first ones off. Mace embraced his sister and took both girls up off the dock into his arms.

"Mena," he said, "these aren't the same girls you had. Where did you get them?"

The girls laughed and kissed Mace on the cheek.

"Uncle Mace, we're growing up is all!"

"You'd be Millicent," he said, looking at the smaller of the two. "Right?"

"No, I'm Millicent," the older one said, pounding his broad shoulders with her fists. "She is Martha!"

"Oh," Mace grinned. "It's going to take me some time to get used to this."

They all laughed as he lowered them back to the pier.

"Mena Vickery, this is Delta Wadsworth," Mace said, introducing the two women. They shook gloved hands and exchanged smiles. "Delta is the daughter of my landlord and owner to the Mercantile."

Not yet having released Mena's hand, Delta said, "I feel as if I've known you for years. Mace has told me so much about you." She looked down at the girls, "And about you two, as well."

Millicent curtsied, and Martha tried her best to copy her big sister's actions.

"Mace has mentioned you in his letters," Mena said. "I'm sure we will be friends."

Mace stepped off to organize the baggage as the women talked.

Claxton Landers stepped up pencil and note pad in hand. "Delta, who are these lovely creatures?"

Delta introduced the reporter to Mena, Millicent, and Martha. "Mrs. Mena Vickery -- Mace's sister."

"I see," Claxton said. "There is a definite family resemblance."

All the bags and boxes were loaded onto a wagon as Mace returned.

"Marshal," Claxton said.

"Claxton," Mace greeted him with a handshake.

"Wonderful family you appear to have here. Where are they going to be residing?"

"North Seventh and M," Mace said as Claxton made a note. "But give them a little time to settle in."

"Oh, I won't print their exact address. But there are ladies in town who will come by my office wanting to know."

"Shall we go," Mace ushered the ladies to a waiting buggy.

"It has been a pleasure," Claxton said, tipping his hat.

* * *

After six cases had been heard and adjudicated, Judge Parker closed court for the day.

Upstairs in his office, District Attorney Rupert Dalby met with Deputy Marshal Cornelius Carney. The stern and unforgiving Dalby had a lean and narrow face, thinning hair, and deep-set eyes. He read the report of the arrest of Eben Snee, the half Cherokee, and half German-American, who had confessed to a twin murder. After he finished the document, Dalby looked up at the imposing Deputy Carney.

"You brought him in?"

"He's downstairs in the jail right now," Carney answered.

Dalby shuffled to a second document.

"I'm going to need more than this."

"It's a witnessed confession," the Deputy said. "I had Sheriff Barrows sign it, too."

"Not enough," Dalby said, flopping into his creaking chair. "Where are the bodies of —," he looked at the last document again, "Harmon Stilegebouer and his wife?"

"He said he dropped them off in a crevice in the Arbuckle Mountains near their house."

"I need the bodies — or so parts of them that can prove murder."

"Oh, shit," Carney said. "All right. I'll go back and find the bodies."

"Have you met the new Marshal? He wants to meet all the Deputies when they come in."

"He'll have to wait til' I come back with the bodies you need." Carney left in a huff.

"I don't think Marshal Truax is going to like that. Before you do anything else, go down the hall and meet the Marshal."

Frustrated and fuming, Carney did as Rupert Dalby advised.

What he discovered surprised him. Carney took a liking to Mace, who understood the Deputy's haste to find the bodies.

"I have a suggestion for you if you're interested," Mace said.

"What's that?" Carney said with his temper now under control.

"Do you know, John Browneagle?"

"Yep."

"Find him and get him to go with you. He'll be a good man to help you track down the bodies."

Carney considered the idea a moment and admitted, "That's a good idea, Marshal. I'll do that."

* * *

Emery Haguse was surprised when he rounded a bend in the dusty road to find two Deputy Marshals, both with guns drawn, waiting for him. Haguse was twenty-four and just able to grow thin sideburns. His baby face sported a few hairs but could not produce much in the way of facial hair. He was a soft man who didn't display any signs of hard work.

He pulled his sorrel to a halt and raised his hands.

"Emery Haguse?" one of the Marshals asked.

"Yes," he said slowly.

Deputy Marshal Larnin Fixsen looked to be about the same age as Haguse. The Marshal held his revolver steady as he dismounted and approached Haguse. The peace officer wore a sombrero, denim, and boots with spurs. He pulled Haguse's gun from the man's holster and checked to make sure the arrested man had no other weapons on him.

"What's this all about?" Haguse asked, trying to appear as innocent as possible.

"Wilber Gabel," the other Marshal, Zeno Lope, a few years older than his partner, said still mounted with a double-barrel shotgun aimed at the young rider.

"What about, Wilber?" Haguse asked. His left eye developed a nervous twitch.

"He's dead," Marshal Lope said. "Get off your horse and empty your pockets."

Haguse stepped down and pulled out a few coins from one of his pants' pockets.

"The coat, too," Marshal Fixsen said, checking Haguse's hand. "What's this?" The Marshal picked out a coin, which had an Indian symbol stamped into a silver concho. He flipped it over. "'WG' it says on the back," Fixsen said to Marshal Lope.

"For Wilber Gabel," Lope said. "Just like the students said."

From inside his coat pocket, Haguse produced a wad of paper currency. Fixsen took the money and looked at it. "Looks like a traveling teacher's pay for a whole year."

Haguse swallowed but said nothing.

Marshal Lope said, "Emery Haguse, you are under arrest for the robbery and murder of Wilber Gabel."

"Mount up, Haguse. This is going to be your last ride," Fixsen said after putting handcuffs on the killer.

"Judge Parker will have something special for you," Marshal Fixsen said.

"A trip up thirteen steps," Zeno Lope added, "— then a short drop straight to hell."

# CHAPTER 5

"I love my brother, and I know he loves us," Mena Vickery said to her new fast friend, Delta Wadsworth. The two women were sitting at the breakfast table having tea while Mena's daughter, four-year-old Martha, played in the back yard. "But it's not his job to support us. I need to find something to do to bring in some money. We need to be able to stand on our own."

"They're not looking for a school teacher? You said you'd taught before."

"Three years before I married, and even every year, since. But there are no vacancies in town," Mena said, brushing a stray curl of her dark blonde hair from her forehead. "I'd have to travel to one of the outlying schools and with the girls to take care of that's more than I can manage."

"So, you're still looking in town?"

Mena glanced down at a copy of the Ft. Smith Ledger on the table. "I am. But the only want ads are for things men can do."

Delta took another sip of her tea. She was thoughtful and squinted her deep brown eyes. "I'll keep my ears open at the store. If I hear of anything, I'll come right to you."

"Thanks," Mena said, patting Delta's hand.

"But I'm sure Mace doesn't mind the situation. He's said as much to me. He's concerned for you and the girls."

"I know he is."

"And he's making more money than he's ever made. The Marshal's position pays better than being a major in the Army. And he's not a big spender."

"Yes, but I'm sure Mace blames himself somewhat for Benson 's death. He was a lieutenant and Mace assigned him to lead the patrol that was attacked. Of course, it's not Mace's fault. It was Benson 's turn, and he was more than happy to go."

"Mace has never mentioned that — but I knew something was bothering him about your husband's death. That must be it."

"It wasn't Mace's fault, and I never blamed him."

The two women sipped their tea in silence for a moment before Mena said, with a wink, "But, should he decide to settle down with someone he loves — things would change. And they should."

"They're not headed in that direction," Delta said. "Well, not in any hurry, anyway. It's only been a little over a year since I lost Ely."

"Have you ever thought about trying to rebuild your hotel? Ft. Smith keeps growing?"

"I've thought about it. Father has offered to help finance one. But after the fire — even a new hotel would bring back memories I'm not sure I want."

"I can understand that."

"Speaking of school, how does Millicent like it?"

"She loves it. I think the kids have shortened her name to 'Milly' — and she likes it."

"What's with all the m's in your names. Mace, Mena, Millicent — Milly — and Martha?"

"It was something my parents liked. Papa's name was Mark, and momma was Matie."

* * *

The Dove House was the second of two houses of ill-repute owned by Jewell Bach. The four-foot nine-inch beauty dressed elegantly and spoke as if she were eastern educated and brought up in a wealthy home. She possessed an enticing figure, light grey eyes set against porcelain skin and coal-black hair.

Her girls were all clean and well mannered even if, in this second house, they dressed to seduce. One of her regular customers had become Stoney Walsh, a Deputy Marshal and official hangman for Judge Parker's Court. He had stopped wearing his worn-out Confederate uniform since he had a steady income. Stony refused to wear anything in blue, choosing a new outfit of tan instead. At thirty-seven, the former rebel soldier was missing his left leg from the knee down. He walked using a wooden peg leg.

Surprisingly, it was his missing leg, which made Stony popular with the women who plied their trade on their backs. He would hang around even after getting his ashes hauled and visit with the girls. He was a good storyteller and always made them laugh.

Stony got to his feet when Jewell Bach stepped into the parlor to check on her establishment.

"Miss Bach," he said, tipping his hat.

"Stony," she smiled. "You are a man of amazing stamina, I'm told."

"I do my best, ma'am," he said, trying not to blush.

"It is always good to see you," she said, turning to go.

"Miss Bach," Stony stopped her. "Could you do me a favor?"

She turned back to him, cocking her head. "It all depends on what it is. You know I am very exclusive."

"Oh, no ma'am," Stony said. "It's nothin' like that. I was hopin' you'd spread the word that -- that I've decided I want to be called' Stonewall.' Seein' as how I'm a proper lawman and all."

"Stonewall," she said, letting the words slip off her tongue. "I believe I can oblige you."

"It'd be much appreciated," he said.

"Mr. Stonewall Welch, it is from now on," she smiled.

"Thank you, ma'am."

Jewell walked off down the hall, and Stonewall sat back down with the three doves he'd been visiting with. The Professor, a black piano player, bartender, and bouncer, began playing an upbeat tune.

The front door opened, and three men in their thirties entered.

Two of them wore deputy marshal badges. The Professor looked over his shoulder and spoke but continued to play.

"Welcome to The Dove House. What is your pleasure?"

"Nookie," the biggest of the three said, and his partners laughed.

The Professor ended his tune and rose to face the three.

"Marshals Fremont Sauls, Marshal Monte Oker. Mr. Gee Plank, I believe."

"Good memory, Professor," Fremont said. He was almost six feet tall with a thick neck and large hands. He was a filthy looking man who, from his smell, much needed a bath.

Monte Oker was overweight and had food stains down the front of his shirt.

Their wagon driver, Gee Plank, not a Marshal but still on the Court's payroll, was missing teeth. Those that were left were stained, and he had a wad of tobacco in his cheek.

Fremont noticed Stonewall's badge. "Who are you?"

"Stonewall Walsh. Deputy Marshal and hangman."

"We heard of you," Oker said through his flabby lips. "You do a better job than the last one."

The three girls got to their feet, put on their professional smiles, and each went to one of the three men.

"Have you three seen Marshal Truax?" Stonewall asked.

"Nope," said Fremont. "And we don't intend to until we get our knobs polished — real good."

As the pairs trooped up the stairs, Stonewall stood up, picked up his hat, and nodded to the Professor as he left.

# CHAPTER 6

"Mr. Cross?" Mace spoke to Judge Parker's clerk, who had just delivered a stack of warrants to the Marshal's desk.

Presley Cross, late '30s, short, with thin, blonde hair, turned back to Mace.

"Ft. Smith is the county seat of Sebastian County, isn't it?" Mace asked.

"It is — but so is Van Buren."

"Two county seats?"

"The only one I know of in the nation, sir."

"Do we have a county sheriff?"

"The last one died several months ago. His two deputies quit, and a replacement has not been named. I expect someone will run for the office in this November's election."

"Do we have a town marshal?"

"There's been no call for one. With so many Deputy U.S. Marshals around and now with you as Marshal, no one has sought one."

"But we officially only enforce federal laws. What about state laws and city ordinances?"

"It's usually one of our Deputy Marshals who steps in when one is required."

"Is Judge Parker all right with this?"

"We've not discussed it."

"Since you have his ear more than I do, would you please mention to him that I would like to see about getting some local and state law enforcement. Our deputies should not be meddling in either one — except as private citizens."

"I'll mention it. But I think you are the one who needs to make the case. I'll put you on his calendar for tomorrow night after court. How is that for you?"

"Fine. I'll be here."

Cross returned to his office, and Mace picked up the new warrants. As he read the charges and the locations, he sorted them into stacks. He was interrupted by a tap on his door. Looking up, he found Deputy Marshals Larnin Fixsen and Zeno Lope. Fixsen held his a sombrero in his hand. The mid-twenties lawman was dressed in denim. Beside him, Lope, about thirty, kept his sweat-stained hat on.

"You wanted to see us, Marshal?" the older of the pair said.

Mace got to his feet and extended his hand. "Mace Truax, he said."

The older man took Mace's hand, saying, "Zeno Lope."

"Larnin Fixsen," the younger man said, accepting Mace's hand.

"You two brought in Emery Haguse, right?"

"For killing his friend Wilber Gabel — a traveling teacher," Fixsen said.

"I hear good things about you, gentlemen," Mace said.

"Don't make the mistake of thinking of us as *gentlemen*," Zeno Lope said. "We're hard, mean sons-of-bitches."

"But honest and faithful to your job," Mace added with a smile.

The two Deputies looked at each other before Fixsen turned back to Mace. "Don't know any other way t' be, Marshal."

"I understand," Mace said. "That's why I wanted to meet you. I've been out there — I know what you're up against. You may not know it or even believe it, but you men are making history — and making The Nations a better place to live."

Neither Deputy knew what to say. After a moment, Lope said, "Nobody's ever said that about what we do."

"That's why I wanted you to know. How long will you be in town? I'd like to have a drink with you both."

"Long enough to testify," Fixen said.

"And we hope we're back to see him hung," Lope added.

* * *

The Red Eye saloon catered to a rougher crowd than The Sidewheeler. It was a favorite for Deputy Marshals. It was where Mace arranged to meet Deputies Zeno Lope and Larnin Fixsen for a drink — but that was later in the week. At the moment Mace was at the bar drinking a beer when Fremont, Oker, and Plank pushed their way in. The trio had finished their business at The Dove House and now bellied up to the bar and ordered whiskey.

Mace put down his mug and stepped down.

"Fremont, Oker, and Plank."

The men looked over at Mace.

"The new Marshal, boys," Fremont said. "Guess we're not going to have to look him up."

"You knew I wanted to see you as soon as you came to town?"

"Yeah, we heard," Fremont looked at his partners. Back to Mace, he said, "But we have our own way of doing things, Marshal. That's the good thing about this job."

"You'll not have to worry about that anymore. Turn in your badges?"

"Turn in our —." Oker started and stopped.

"Put them down on the bar."

The three men looked from one to the other. Fremont turned to face Mace. Oker stepped out beside Fremont and dropped his hand to his waist. Mace could see Plank between the two of them.

"If you're tryin' t' fire us — *Marshal*," Fremont spat, "you're going to have to make it permanent."

"It is permanent," Mace said. "I know your record. You go out with warrants and come back with an empty wagon. You report the men you were after as dead and buried."

"You calling us liars," Oker snarled.

"There are reports of the men you supposedly killed turning up in Texas, Kansas, and Colorado. Not dead at all. I don't think I need to go searching for empty graves, do you?"

Mace pulled his coat back behind him, clearing his pistol for a fight.

Fremont went for his gun, and so did Oker.

Mace had both his Schofields before either Fremont or Oker could even get theirs out of their holsters. Mace's second pistol, the one Temple Morgan had suggested he wear under his coat behind him, was a shock neither Deputy expected. Oker froze, but Fremont didn't stop. Mace shot him in the center of his chest.

Plank seemed to freeze in place. He, like Oker, understood if they made a move they'd join Fremont dead on the sawdust-covered floor of the Red Eye saloon.

"Hands up," Mace directed Oker and Plank. "With your left hand, untie the pig line around your leg and unbuckle your gunbelts. Let them drop to the floor."

Both men complied.

"Badge on the bar," Mace told Oker. The man removed his badge as directed.

"Get out of Ft. Smith and the Territory. Don't ever come back."

"How about our pay?" Oker asked.

"I'm sure you have collected more than enough for those empty graves.

"We'll need our guns," Plank said.

"You have other guns," Mace said. "Leave these here. You have thirty minutes to get out of town, or I am arresting you."

The duo stepped around Mace and went to the door. As Plank moved, Mace saw Stonewall standing behind where the man had stood. Stonewall slipped the Arkansas toothpick he had been holding against Plank's back in its sheath.

"Thank you," Mace said, holstering his pistols.

"My pleasure, Marshal. I'll get the undertaker to collect the trash," Stonewall said, referring to Fremont. "I'll fetch the guns and badges up to your office."

"I'm obliged — Stonewall."

# CHAPTER 7

Claxton Landers, owner/publisher/editor/reporter for the <u>Ft.
Smith Daily Ledger</u> had lunch with the new Marshal. They
met a block from the courthouse at Ma Nauman's Cafe after
the morning rush.

The newspaperman parked his bowler hat on the empty chair next
to him and pushed his wire-rimmed glasses up on his nose. Besides the
mug of coffee in front of him, Landers had a notepad open. He was
making notes with a short pencil.

The new Marshal sat back in his chair opposite the reporter and
sipped his coffee.

"First question, Marshal, why did you take this job?"

"It seemed to suit me. My experience in the Army, commanding
men, and doing the needed administration gave me what I needed."

"But you went out with a Lighthorse Policeman —," Lander flipped
through his notebook to locate his notes, "— John Browneagle, into
The Nations before you sat down behind the desk. Why did you do
that?"

"I never had respect for an officer above me in the Army who
hadn't done what he expected the men below him to do. I needed to
find out what the Deputies and the Lighthorse were up against."

"And did you learn?"

"Yes. There are things experience can teach you nothing else can. John Browneagle didn't make it easy on me — I didn't want him to. Now I have a grasp of the downright evil and the danger the men who serve Judge Parker's court face daily."

Landers scribbled for a moment before he looked up and asked, "What is your background, Marshal?"

"The Army. I came out of West Point and requested duty here in the West."

"Why?"

"My parents were killed in an Indian raid. They were settlers in Texas."

"Would it be accurate to say you went into the Army seeking revenge?"

Mace slowly nodded his head. "At first — in the early days of my service."

"You changed your mind?"

"Studying history — and watching our dealing with the different tribes gave me a different perspective."

"How so?"

"As white men, we are not better or any worse than any other race. How do you think we would respond to people — from anywhere — who came to our country and tried to take what had been our ancestral lands?"

"Is that what we are doing?"

"Isn't it," Mace said, putting his coffee mug down.

"But we make treaties with the Indians — paying them money or offering them other concessions for the land we request?"

"And how often have we reneged on these treaties if not ignored them when more people come — or we discover something like gold on their lands?"

"So you are what many would call an 'Indian lover?'"

"Hardly. The ancient ways of life the Indians practice are savage, brutal, and often based on the theft and killing of others. To be a man in most Indian societies, you must be a warrior — a killer. And your worth is counted in the number of lives you have taken, horses you have stolen and the slaves you have acquired. Most of the tribes have no interest in learning our ways — for farming or for anything else. They don't want to make steel, but they want our steel knives, rifles, and pistols.

"However, the Indians are trying to protect what was once theirs — their land — their ways of life. We are trying to change everything. Unfortunately for the Indians, that's the way the world and history works. The land they claim as theirs was once the land of someone else — until they came and took it away. That's the way it is today and was yesterday. We are on the side of history that is advancing — we are stronger and we outnumber them. For the most part, we're not as savage as the Indians are — but they're responding to the loss of everything they have or have ever had according to their ways. The five Civilized Tribes are accepting the changing times. At least most of them are. Some never will."

"How about your parents? Are you no longer — angry about them?"

"I am — but I've seen and learned more than I knew when they died. They didn't die for nothing — they thought they had the rights to the land they were on — they had bought it — and they were defending it. They were attacked by people who were frustrated and knew no other way to respond except to kill."

A waitress came by and refilled the mugs of both men before she moved on.

"Are you a religious man, Marshal?"

"In my own way. I am not the first to attend church — but I believe in God and the example of Jesus Christ. I hope I'm a fair and honorable man. I do my best to be so. And yet I've taken on a job that involves violence to the point of killing. My faith is the practice of the Golden Rule — as it applies to those who are beastly and cruel — and have neither faith or honor.

"The truth I have come to understand is that some men will never live in peace nor allow others to do so. The law Judge Parker is trying to bring to The Indian Territory is the same law we live by. We can never have peace with any tribe until we prove we can be trusted to keep our word and to live justly. That's where we Marshals come in.

Our job is not to be judge and jury but to bring suspected criminals into court where all sides can be heard — and hopefully, justice can be done."

"You know that the Judge and the Marshal before you and Judge Parker were neither just nor honest?"

"Yes. And to be trusted, we have to earn the respect of people who have learned not to trust any white man — especially one with a badge and a gun. It is a hard job — and a lonely one. Those before us have made our jobs harder. None of us on this side on the law expected it to be easy. But it's a job that has to be done — and done with honesty, truth, and even compassion."

"Does that explain your gunfight with former Marshals Fremont Sauls and Monte Oker?"

"It didn't have to come to that. But they are not the kind of men the Judge wants wearing badges and representing our honor and justice."

"One last question, Marshal. Are you ready to die for this job?"

"We're all going to die, Mr. Landers. We can't always choose the when or the how. All we can do is try to make our lives count for something — and hopefully the same will be said of our death. If I am killed in this job — as long as I do it the way I hope I am, I will be satisfied."

# CHAPTER 8

"Oyez! Oyez!" Bailiff Hershel Adrian called out to the courtroom. The Honorable Court for the Western District of Arkansas, having jurisdiction over the Indian Territory, is now in session. His Honor, Judge Issac Parker, presiding."

Adrian had been Sebastian County Sheriff until he was wounded, arresting a thief. The solidly built middle-aged man recovered but found himself hesitant toward his job. He'd retired. However, only a few weeks of fishing and having little else to do, his wife of seventeen years told him to get out of *her* house and get a job — and not to come home until supper time.

Judge Parker opened the back door to the courtroom and took the bench. He pounded his gavel twice.

"Call the first item," the Judge said.

"Arraignment of Kerwood Wannamaker on the charge of murder," the Court Clerk, Presley Cross, read, handing the Judge the Charge Sheet. "All parties are present, Your Honor."

"Mr. Dalby," the Judge addressed the dower District Attorney.

Rupert Dalby stood at the prosecution table looking up at Judge Parker through deep-set, narrow eyes.

"Mr. Kerwood Wannamaker is charged with the murder of his wife of two years, Leta Golden Flower Wannamaker. He shot her in the back. The Prosecution requests that Mr. Wannamaker be held until a date is set for his trial."

"Was the victim white or Indian?" Judge Parker wanted to know.

"She was white but had been captured from her home in Texas at twelve years of age. She was married to an Arapahoe brave before she was returned to white society. She claimed to be Arapahoe."

"Defense?"

"Your Honor, Mr. Wannamaker turned himself into Marshal Truax and has admitted his part in the crime," attorney Temple Houston said, standing in his all-white attire.

"How do you plead Mr. Wannamaker?"

Kerwood stood and spoke with a clear, confident voice. The fit and successful rancher said, "Not guilty by reason of justifiable homicide."

"The defense requests bail and that Mr. Wannamaker be remanded to my custody," Houston said.

"Your honor," Dalby said, straining not to raise his voice, "the charge is murder. The Prosecution respectfully requests that this defendant be treated like every other murder suspect and jailed."

"If it please the Court," Temple Houston said calmly, "Mr. Wanna-maker has not fled justice. Indeed he has voluntarily surrendered himself to it. He is a successful rancher, owner of the Circle W East of Van Buren. He is a long time resident of Arkansas, has a son back on the ranch, and has no intention of taking flight."

Judge Parker thought for a moment before he said, "The defendant's plea is hereby accepted, and bond is set at three-thousand dollars."

"Three thousand?" Attorney Houston said in surprise.

"See the Bailiff to post bond."

Rupert Dalby was disgusted but knew to hold his tongue.

"Your Honor," Houston said, "we would request a little time to gather witnesses and bring them back to Ft. Smith."

"Granted," Judge Parker said. "The Court Clerk will set a reasonable date for the trial."

"Thank you, Your Honor." The defense attorney looked at his client as he said, "About the amount of bail, Your Honor."

The defendant raised a hand to stop any protest from his attorney and nodded his acceptance of bail.

"Yes?" the Judge asked.

"Nothing, Your Honor. Thank you."

Together Wannamaker and Houston crossed to Hershel Adrian, where Houston wrote a check.

"We can go directly to your bank," Wannamaker said, "and I'll have the funds to reimburse you transferred today."

"Let's get a date for trial set," Houston told Wannamaker as they stepped over to the Court Clerk. "And our trip to the bank will have to wait a while. I have another client."

"Next case," Judge Parker said when Houston and Court Clerk , Mr. Cross, were finished.

"The United States of America," the Court Clerk read from the paper in front of him, "vs. Mrs. Belle Starr on the charge of horse theft."

Attorney Houston looked up as a woman in a long dress, but her hands in cuffs went with the Bailiff to the defense table. She was about thirty, with dark hair which matched her eyes. The Bailiff uncuffed her, and she stood to wait for Houston.

The lawyer said a couple of quiet words to Kerwood Wannamaker, who left the courtroom. Houston crossed back to the defense table, shook hands with Mrs. Starr, and then shuffled through his papers until he found the folder he sought.

\* \* \*

"Are the Prosecution and Defense ready," Judge Parker asked?

"Yes," Rupert Dalby said.

"We are, Your Honor," Houston said.

"Proceed."

Dalby read from the charge sheet he lifted from the table. "Mrs. Belle Starr is charged with the theft and sale of a horse belonging to Mr. Jilson Panghorn. The animal in question is a chestnut Morgan, fifteen hands tall and valued at one hundred and thirty dollars. The horse was stolen from Mr. Panghorn's pasture and sold by Mrs. Starr to a Cherokee, Mr. Samuel Vann. Deputy Marshal Cornelius Carney arrested Mrs. Starr and brought back the animal in question as evidence. Both Mr. Panghorn and Mr. Vann are present and ready to testify."

"Mr. Houston?" Judge Parker inquired.

"This whole case is a matter of misunderstanding, Your Honor. Mrs. Starr did not steal the horse in question but purchased it in good faith from a man named Ed Shirly. We have the bill of sale here." Houston held up a quarter of a standard page of paper with handwriting on it. "Mrs. Starr did sell the horse to Mr. Vann — but she did so believing she had the legal right to do so.

"Now that my client realized the mistake, she is willing to reimburse Mr. Vann for the money he paid for the horse."

"Does that satisfy Mr. Vann," the Judge asked.

"Yes," the farmer said from the gallery. "As long as I get my horse back."

"Does the prosecution have any evidence that Mrs. Starr is the one who stole Mr. Panghorn's Morgan?"

"Uh —," the Prosecutor stuttered, " — no we do not, Your Honor. It was the circumstances of the disappearance of the horse and Mrs. Starr's sale of it that lead to the assumption of the theft."

"Due to the lack of evidence, is the Prosecution, therefore, willing to drop the horse-stealing charge?" asked Judge Parker.

Dalby was unhappy, but even in his frustration, he had little choice. "Yes, Your Honor. The Prosecution withdraws the charge."

"Mrs. Starr, please pay Mr. Vann in front of the Baliff — and the horse is ordered returned to Mr. Panghorn. Charges are dismissed." The Judge banged his gavel.

# CHAPTER 9

Ned Christi, a full-blooded Cherokee, attended an Executive Tribal Council meeting the day after the Cherokee Women's Seminary burned to the ground. Long haired Christi had a sparse goatee, unusual for an Indian, and was known for his strong stance for tribal sovereignty.

There was never any suspicion of arson. However, the result of the fire was the complete destruction of the multi-building facility. The council, meeting in Tahlequah, capital of the Cherokee Nation in the foothills of the Ozark Mountains, decided that the school must be rebuilt.

Christi, both a gunsmith and blacksmith, planned to head West-ward toward his home in Wauhillau, less than a dozen miles from Still-well. But first, Christi crossed a nearby creek and bought some liquor from a woman named Sally Shell. The manufacture or sale of liquor in the Indian Territory was against the law. By nature, the American Indians had a low tolerance for alcohol. This, however, didn't mean Indian men and women didn't desire, seek out, and indulge in such spirits.

His low level of endurance for the effects of liquor showed itself when Christi found himself no longer able to ride. He dismounted and slept in the bushes near the creek.

Unknown to Christi, a U.S. Deputy Marsha Dan Maples was on the trail of illegal alcohol sellers. Maples crossed the same creek Christi had, and the same near where Christi was sleeping off the effects of his purchase at Nancy Shell's.

That night Deputy Maples was shot and killed. In the subsequent investigation Ned Christi was named as a possible suspect because he had been in the area. Christi was the only one of the suspects not to be quickly apprehended. The Indian leader only learned about the Deputy Marshal's murder after he had been back in his home for over a week. Christi also learned that he was a suspect in the case.

He was not only literate but aware of the workings of the white man's Court in Ft. Smith and the new "hanging judge" on the bench. Ned Christi, wrote a letter to Judge Parker proclaiming his innocence. Christi had no interest in journeying to the Court and submitting himself to the so-called "justice" there.

With the help and support of other Cherokee, Christi avoided capture for five years. Friends and neighbors even helped the man they admired build what was called a castle. This fortified position in the mountains between two propionate boulders, had a cabin erected behind a defensive wall. Both the outer wall and the walls of the dwelling were double. Large rocks and sand filled the space between the inner and outer walls. The position oversaw any approaching riders and provided shelter for Christi and anyone who joined him.

Still, the Marshals from Ft. Smith wanted to capture Christi. Any crime committed in the area was assigned to Christi. Soon he was thus known by the whites and Court in Ft. Smith as a notorious outlaw.

In one attempt to capture him, Christi wounded a Deputy Marshal. The man didn't die of his wounds, but he was forced to retire from the Court unable to use his left arm.

Mace Truax gave a new warrant to capture Ned Christi to Deputy Jacob Yost. Yost put together a posse of fifteen. With a thousand-dollar reward on Christi's head, the posse attracted bounty hunters as well as ten other Marshals. Yost also acquired a small cannon to storm Ned Christi's castle.

* * *

Following her trial before Judge Parker, Belle Starr returned to Younger Bend, the Indian Territorial hideout and refuge for outlaws and members of the Starr clan. She was welcomed back and her status rose again. She had already achieved a reputation as a legal fixer among the band of miscreants there. Earlier, she had seen to the destruction of moonshine stored as evidence against her second husband, Uriah Starr, and freed him for a lack of evidence. She was smart enough to hire the best lawyers available, Temple Houston in both her and her husband's cases.

Of course, she had stolen the horse she was charged with stealing, but by reimbursing the farmer to whom she had sold the horse for what he had paid her, she was freed from Judge Parker's court. She knew no one witnessed her taking the Morgan at the time of the theft.

Belle was the child of John Shirley, a former Carthage, Missouri blacksmith, inn owner, and county judge and his third wife. Judge Shirley had help from and build the Carthage Female Academy which Belle attended. There she learned to play piano but had a fascination for horses and guns. She became an excellent horsewoman and dead shot with pistol or rifle.

The movement of John Brown moved her as blood was being shed between abolitionist Kansas and proslavery Missouri. She was fifteen when Quantrill's raiders sacked and burned Lawrence Kansas. Quantrill had built a band of hard riding, disciplined raiders and killers. The cream of the group was Cole and Bob Younger, Frank and Jesse James. Althoughs he had not met any of them, Belle idolized these men as heroes.

Her brother Ed led his own band of bushwackers which operated out of Carthage. He was killed and much of the town of Carthage burned to the ground by Federal Troops in 1863. It was her dead brother's name, Ed Shirly, Belle used for the forged bill of sale for the stolen horse for which she faced horse theft charges before Judge Parker.

It was after her brother's death that Belle strapped on two guns and rode off to join the guerrillas. She became a spy for the rebels. Several Yankee soldiers were murdered in broad daylight based on information

Belle supplied. A few months later, Federal troops raided Carthage again, and finished off the town — including the Belle's family home and her father's business.

Her father, John Shirley, moved the family to Texas starting again east of Dallas near Mesquite as a farmer. He placed Belle back in school even while making the new family farm as an outlaw sanctuary.

It was then that Belle met and fell in love with twenty-year-year old Cole Younger. He came to Texas after his gang escaped the law in Missouri. This was 1867 two years after the war was over. When he left, Belle was pregnant — and she never saw him again.

Cole and Bob Younger were wounded and captured in a raid of the banks of Northfield, Minn. Frank and Jesse James escaped. The Youngers were sentenced to life terms in a prison in Stillwater Oklahoma Indian Territory.

Belle next set her cap for Weaver Reed, a little known but prolific horse thief around Dallas. Much to her father's displeasure, his daughter married Reed. When Belle's daughter was born, she was named Pearl. This was when Belle left the child in the care of her parents and went to work in the saloon world of Dallas. She sang, danced, dealt monte, faro and poker. She dressed in eye catching outfits but which were still modest. During those days, Belle did very well financially.

Weaver and Belle took Pearl back to Missouri. Weaver soon became part of a large group of horse thieves who preyed Texas herds, running the stolen stock north. It was after Weaver murdered two brothers suspected of being responsible for killing Reed's brother that Belle and Weaver fled to California. There Belle had a second child, a boy, Ed. It wasn't long, however, that the law on the West Coast was looking for Reed in connection with a stage hold up near San Diego. The family fled back to Texas. It was here that Weaver was killed. This was the event which drew Belle to Younger Bend on the Canadian River in the Cherokee part of the Indian lands.

# CHAPTER 10

Railroads had a powerful impact on The Nations. The Indian Territory was configured as the land which would years later become the Territory and finally the state of Oklahoma. It was 1824 when Congress then marked acreage for the Cherokee, Chickasaw, Choctaw, Creek, and Seminoles. These were the tribes labeled the "Five Civilized Tribes."

The idea from the government was a specified refuge for individual Indian tribes. Tribes who had been persecuted by whites in the eastern United States were granted land that was to be theirs forever. Existing white state governments with additional money from the federal treasury relocated the designated tribes off their ancestral land and moved them to the Indian Territory. From 1828 to 1842, different tribes settled in the newly identified Indian Territory.

These emigrant tribes each reestablished their respective governments, courts of law, and schools. They also each controlled their cultural and social structures according to their heritage or new realities. These "Civilized Tribes" held the title to their lands. The U.S. government recognized the respective tribes and their unique governments. The national government even set up trade with the separate tribes.

Congress also specified that the first railroad to reach the southern Kansas border, near the town of Chetopah, was to have the right to cross through Oklahoma. The Missouri, Kansas, and Texas (MKT or Katy) won the race.

A land grant in the Indian Territory was the prize. However, as the government often does, they changed the rules and the award. The Katy Railroad claims were dumped. The reason given was that some tribal governments had worked with the Confederacy during the Civil War. The U.S. Government forced all of the Five Civilized Tribes to sign new treaties in 1866.

Even though it was the Katy line to make it through the Neosho Valley in Kansas to the Indian Territory, the Atlantic and Pacific (A&P) had already entered The Nations by another path. This one was sixty-eight miles East from Pierce City, Missouri. The A&P laid track into the Territory town of Vinita.

Problems arose with the Five Civilized Tribes, which asserted their treaty sovereignty rights. The problems with the federal government assured land grants for the railroads, caused the A&P to halt where it was. The KTY continued to Texas by bowing to tribal claims and restrictions. Soon cattle from Texas and grain from the north passed through the sparsely populated route. It took the Katy until 1872 to reach Texas and cross the Red River. There wasn't much business conducted in The Nations, but the tracks across it were very productive.

The railroads brought in both many whites and alcohol. Railroad men, as well as traders and other businessmen, quickly came to an understanding. The white men realized that their best bet for working with the Indians was to marry into the tribe. As the husband of a native, a man had access to rent and use tribal lands. This became the key to white mixing with the Indians of The Territory.

The rub came when a criminal case involved a white and an Indian. The charter of the Federal Court for the Western District of Arkansas stipulated that Indian on Indian crime was a matter for tribal laws and courts. But any case involving a white with an Indian fell under the jurisdiction of Judge Parker's court.

\* \* \*

Esau Falzon established a general store at the first MKT passenger and cargo stop in The Nations. The town was named Coo-y-yah, which meant "place of huckleberries" in Cherokee. The MKT changed the name to Pryor Creek. A second stop in Vinita was where the A&P had terminated its operations. Both locations were in the northeast Indian Territory.

The twenty-seven-year-old merchant married a seventeen-year-old Cherokee named Amadahy. It was not a blissful marriage. Falzon considered himself handsome and a magnet to women. He sported a thin but dark mustache that he kept well-trimmed. Flazon frequented cathouses and openly flirted with other women who visited his stores. He dressed in a flashy waistcoat with a gold chain to his pocket watch.

As his marriage deteriorated, Falzon took out his displeasures with his wife, striking her with his hand and his belt. The winsome bride had the sympathy of whites but little from her tribe. She was, after all, a wife and the property of her husband.

Amadahy, the dark-haired, slender but shapely young woman, was abandoned for weeks at a time. Falzon split his time between his two stores. Falzon also saw to the farming of the acreage, which came his way by virtue of his Cherokee marriage.

A telegraph operator and freight manager, thirty-one-year-old Authur Lundy, became her most supportive friend. Blonde and average in every way, Lundy was not attractive but was far from ugly. He first encountered Amadahy on the street a day after she has suffered a beating from her husband. Falzon had used the buckle end of his belt as his primary weapon.

Lundy was shocked at the sight of the young woman and insisted on taking her to a doctor who treated her abrasions and bruises. He took her home and fixed her a meal before he left. The railroad man continued to check on her for the rest of the week.

When Falzon finally returned, he took no notice of the significant improvement of his wife's condition. The situation between the pair didn't change, and Amadahy endured other beatings over the next month.

Authur Lundy confronted Falzon after discovering Amadahy, mistreated again. Lundy came prepared for a fight with Falzon, but the husband didn't seem to care enough.

"You want to take care of the slut," he told Lundy, "be my guest. I've gotten what I wanted out of her." With that, Falzon strolled off.

Lundy did take in Amadahy, and soon the two found a fondness which quickly heightened to love. Although they were living in sin, no one seemed to mind — especially Esau Falzon.

The men spoke when the two met at the train terminal before Falzon was taking another trip from Pryor Creek down to his second store at a stop called Gibson Station.

"How are you liking her?" Falzon asked.

"You are a bastard, Falzon," Lundy said.

"Oh, I may be. But I'm glad to let you use my wife. She's still *my* wife. I am not going to divorce her. You are welcome to have her for anything else you like." He started to board the train when he stopped and searched his pockets. Finally, he reached inside his coat and produced a small envelope.

"By now, you should know she sometimes has trouble sleeping — no matter how well you screw her. When that happens, give her some of this in her tea. It will help her sleep."

Lundy eyed the packet suspiciously.

"Don't worry about it. It's harmless." Falzon stepped up on the train. "You can take some yourself. You'll see."

# CHAPTER 11

Mena and Martha, her younger daughter, walked down the street of Ft. Smith toward Keeling's Mercantile, Delta's father's store, when they passed the office of the <u>Ledger</u>. She noticed a copy of the paper's Friday edition taped to the office window. Before they were past it, Mena stopped and turned around. Keeping Martha's hand in hers, the two retraced their steps and went into the newspaper building.

The thirty-four-year-old owner/reporter/editor, Claxton Landers, was selecting type from a drawer of lead fonts. He happened to be shaved this day. Usually, he would go several days between shaves. Claxton looked over his wire-rimmed glasses and put down his work.

"Good morning," he said cheerfully. "What can I do for you?"

"I think it's a question of what I can do for you, Mr. Landers."

"Oh? How's that?"

"You're obviously a well-read and educated man — your paper reflects that."

"Thank you. Praise is always appreciated."

"But are you aware of the number of errors — grammatical, spelling, and punctuation — your paper contains in each edition?"

Ledger ran he hand over his balding head and leaned back a little as he reacted to Mena's remark.

"You don't say."

"I do say. I expect you've heard people talk about this before. It can't be a surprise. And you must be aware of it, at least to some degree, yourself."

"I do the very best I can, Mrs. Vickery."

"I'm sure you do, sir."

"Then what are you saying?"

"That you need someone to check your work. Your papers will one day be historical documents. What is it they say, 'Newspapers are the first draft of history?' Something like that. It will be ashamed if historians think you were lazy or careless."

"I am neither, thank you, madam!"

"Then, I'm saying you should have a — I don't know what you call such a position, but I'm positive every sizeable newspaper has one."

"It's a copy editor. And this is not a sizeable operation. I'm a one-man-band."

"But growing. And as much as I disagree with the content of your competitor, The Vindicator doesn't seem to have the same problems. At least not to the same degree."

"Believe it or not, Joseph Pickering is married. It's his wife who double-checks his copy."

"Then, you should either get you a wife, Mr. Claxton, or employ a — copy editor."

Claxton was silent for a moment and then smiled as he said, "Are you proposing, Mrs. Vickery, or applying for a job?"

"What would such a position pay?"

"I put out two papers a week — Tuesday and Friday. A copy editor would be worth — seventy-five dollars week."

"What would *you* expect to be paid as a copy editor, Mr. Claxton."

"Well, seeing as how I'm a man — with experience — I'd expect to get ninety-five dollars a week. But you, Mrs. Vickery..."

He didn't get to finish his thought because Mena cut him off. "Is it obvious what the sex is of a copy editor by what is on the page?"

"No, but a man, a head of a household would be expected ..."

Mena lifted Martha off the floor and held her in one arm.

"I am the head of a household, Mr. Claxton. And Martha has a sister — two years older. I am responsible for them."

"But, you are under the care of Marshal Truax."

"I intend to support my family by myself. What if something happens to my brother? And I, too have experience. As a teacher, I expect I've checked and corrected more pages than you've ever printed.

"Mr. Claxton, give me a copy of one of your back issues — one I've not read. If I fail to find less than six errors on the front page, I will accept your seventy-five dollars a week offer. If I find six — or more — you will hire me at ninety-five."

Claxton looked at Mena a moment then with a nod accepted her offer. He found an edition from two months back and offered her a red pencil and a desk. When Mena found seven errors, Claxton sighed.

"You're going to have to learn copyediting marks."

"I think I can do that," Mena said.

"And be here in the office weekdays to take ads."

"That's reasonable."

"And write up the ads — and obituaries."

"I'll begin eight o'clock tomorrow morning," she said, and she left.

Finally, Claxton closed his mouth and sat down. Had he been had or had he made a wise decision. He wasn't sure.

* * *

"Eben Snee's confession ain't good enough?" Sheriff Glover Barrows was in disbelief. "Hell, I heard it. He signed it. I even signed it as a witness."

"The District Attorney, Rupert Dalby, say's he needs more," Deputy Marshal Cornelius Carney said. "He wants the bodies."

Carney and Barrows were in Reno City, Oklahoma Indian Territory. In 1859, the Caddo Indians originally from Lousiana were relocated from their Texas reservation to what would become Canadian County in central Oklahoma. Five-foot eight-inch Indian Territorial Policeman, John Browneagle, stood there, too.

"So, we've got to go up in the mountains and find them?" Barrows said, heaving himself up from his desk chair. He was a steely man with a tight jaw and firm muscles. He was no taller than John Browneagle and carried himself with the same confidence. "Guess we'll have to get back to the Stilegebouer place t' start. John, I'm glad you're with us. You've got better horse sense about tracking than I ever have."

"Marshal Carney asked me to come."

"I have to confess," Carney said, "it was the new Marshal's idea."

"Truax?" Barrows asked.

"Yup."

"How's he working out? I ain't met him, but I hear good things about him."

"So far, so good. I like him," Carney said and then turned to Browneagle. "You rode with him, I hear. What did you think?"

"He wanted to know what this part of the job was like. He held his own."

"Good to know," Carney said. "Let's get about this."

"I expect we'll need some rope, maybe an ax and a bucket if we find them," Sheriff Barrows said. "And since this ain't goin' t' be no picnic, I reckon we ought to grab a bite t' eat 'fore we go. No tellin' how long we'll be out there lookin'."

.

# CHAPTER 12

The three lawmen located the Stilegebouer farm at the edge of the Arbuckle Mountains. They searched for any clues which the weeks and the weather had not obliterated.

Inside the farmhouse, they found most things in good order except for the signs of a struggle and a pool of blood on the kitchen floor. Even the barn was neat and orderly. No horses or other animals were around.

John Browneagle studied the place and walked around the house. He looked up at the beautiful Arbuckle Mountains. Trees were beginning to turn as fall approached. The speckled landscape was basically granite but cut with many creeks and streams.

When the Deputy Marshal joined Browneagle, and Sheriff Barrows, Carney asked the Policeman, "What do you think, John?"

"There are no signs. We should split up and fan out. Each of us takes a slice of this like it was pie. If we find anything, fire two shots in the air and the other two will come."

"At least we don't need to have cold camps," Carney said.

"A good fire would be best," Browneagle said. "There are mountain lions up there."

* * *

Marshal Mace Truax took Delta Wadsworth for a sunset buggy ride. It was now well over a year and a half since her husband, Ely, had died in a hotel fire. It was a gorgeous evening and the purple/pink clouds were a joy to see across the river. They enjoyed each other's company and only headed back to town as darkness began to close in.

Mace pulled the rented buggy up in front of the home Delta shared with her father. He walked her to the front door, and they felt an urge to kiss — but something held them both back. After holding each other's eyes for an awkward moment, Mace smiled and tipped his hat.

He headed back to the livery when gunshots shattered the night air. Mace pulled up and saw two drunk cowboys, sharing a bottle of whiskey, and were howling at the moon. Such disturbances were not in the jurisdiction of federal law enforcement. But there was no one else who would step in.

Mace got down from the buggy and walked up the dirt street to the pair who continued their celebration. He approached the cowboys from behind and used his pistol to coldcock both as they were ready to fire their next shots. Next, the Marshal collected their revolvers and shoved them in his belt. He loaded the two onto the floor of his buggy and turned around, heading for the Mayor's house.

* * *

Mayor Fritz Essleman overtopped his pants. He waddled to the front door carrying his linen napkin in a chubby hand, responding to Mace's rapping on the door frame.

The two drunk and dirty cowboys were lying on the Mayor's front porch. Before Mace could say a word or the Mayor question the interruption of his dinner, one of the cowboys jerked and threw up on the painted boards. As soon as the cowhand's stomach was empty, he dropped back down into his own vomit.

"What the hell?" the Mayor said.

"Ft. Smith needs a town marshal, Mr. Mayor?"

"Town marshal?" Estleman echoed as Mace handed him the

cowboy's pistols. "I don't believe we have the tax base for such an office."

"Then, Sebastian County needs to appoint a sheriff until the next election. Cleaning up the civil disturbances — any civil or state laws — on the streets of Ft. Smith is not the job of U.S. Marshals."

"That's Judge Liddy's affair."

"I didn't collect these two," Mace gestured to the passed out cowboys, "in Van Buren." Van Buren was northeast of Ft. Smith. It was, however, one of the two county seats of Sebastian County. "This is the town's problem — or a deputy sheriff's problem for the county. I expect you, Mr. Mayor, to either get a town marshal, or put pressure on Judge Libby as county judge, to get a sheriff and deputies in place. Until something like that changes, my deputies and I are going to continue to use your front porch as a holding cell."

"What?" the Mayor was flabbergasted.

Mace turned and stepped off to the buggy.

* * *

John Browneagle rode his dappled gray right up the middle of the mountain. Carney took the right portion and Barrows the left.

It took two and a half days of searching before Browneagle fired the signal shots. By late afternoon, after he had fired again to help his partners locate him, Browneagle had a camp set up when first Sheriff Barrows and the Deputy Marshal Carney located him.

"Up here," Browneagle said, as he led the other two men to a crevasse. "At noon, the light was better, and I could see both bodies. Her calico dress was the easiest to spot."

"We're going to need a log across this," Carney said.

"Maybe a small tree," Barrows suggested.

"It will have to be strong if it's going to hold one of us and another body," Browneagle said. "I'll go find one."

"Take the ax off my packhorse," the Sheriff said, still looking down in the narrow crack in the hard rock.

# CHAPTER 13

T he next morning the men laid the log of the tree, eight inches in diameter, across the opening. Barrows tossed the rope over it down into the chasm.

"Who's the lightest one of us?" he asked.

"It's my job," Carney said as he pulled the rope to where he sat on the edge of the fissure. He made a loop, checked that it was secure, and put one boot into it. "Lower away," he said.

It was still dark in the depths of the crack as the Lighthorse Policeman went down. But the closer he got, the clearer the body forms became. Then something moved in the chest of one of them, and a distinct rattling sounded.

"Haul me up!" Carney yelled. "There's rattler's down here!"

Browneagle and Sheriff Barrows pulled hard and brought Carney back up into the daylight.

"They've made a nest in and around the bodies," he told them.

"We're going to need torches," Barrows said.

Browneagle was already off, his bowie knife in his hands looking for what he needed.

Carney mounted up and rode back to the farmhouse. It was midafternoon before he returned. He had rags and a can of coal-oil.

They wrapped the three branches Browneagle had gathered in cloth and soaked them with the flammable liquid. They set one on fire and dropped it on the end where Carney had found the bodies. The Marshal took another flaming stick in his hands as he descended the next time.

The serpents had moved away from what was left of the corpses but were bunched at the other end. About halfway down, Craney tossed his torch between the reptile gathering and the bodies.

"Pull me up. I'll need the other torch!" he called.

When he had the last torch in his hand and was lowered back down the cleft in the rocks, the snakes had disappeared. Carney could see the path they left when they slithered out a tiny opening at the end of the fissure. Using the blanket he brought with him on this trip, the Marshal was able to get the bones and remains close, and the hair of the woman wrapped and secured. Browneagle and Barrows pulled the evidence out and lowered the blanket and the rope once more.

Carney was sweating as he emerged from the fissure when all the body parts that could be recovered were on the granite beside the crack.

"Now if this don't suit Rupert Dalby," Carney said, catching his breath flat on his back, "the som'bitch can come up here and go down that hole himself. And I hope the rattlesnakes come back."

\* \* \*

Mace stood in the lobby of The Sophisticated Lady, his hat in his hand. Jewell Bach, the owner, and madam, of Ft. Smith's most exclusive gentlemen's house of pleasure, came up the hallway from the kitchen to meet the Marshal. The four foot nine inched, ravishing lady with light grey eyes, porcelain skin and coal-black hair, looked curious. She offered her hand.

"Marshal Truax," she said.

"Miss Bach," he said, shaking her hand.

"What can we do for you?"

"I'd like to have a conversation with you if you have the time."

"You certainly chose your time wisely. We don't expect traffic until later this afternoon."

"I expected you might be a late sleeper," Mace said. "But, I hoped this would be a time when you'd have a few minutes to spare."

"Let's go to my office," she said, leading the way past the bottom of the stairs to a closed-door across from the parlor.

She took a seat in a guest chair instead of going behind her desk. She offered another to Mace.

"I'm sure this is not a social visit, Marshal," she smiled. "You and Mrs. Wadsworth have become quite an item I understand."

"No, not your business, anyway," he said, "I came seeking your help and advice."

This took Jewell by surprise. "Please," she asked him to proceed.

"I am looking for men who would make good Deputy Marshals."

"Yes, I've seen your notices in both local papers."

"They're also running in the Little Rock, Kansas City, and Denver papers."

"And you want to know if I can suggest any candidates?"

"That and I'd like for you to keep an eye open in the future. I have over one hundred positions to fill."

"Such men would be more apt to visit my Dover House than here."

"Yes, I would expect so, too."

"Well, Marshal, I'll have to give this some thought. Your criteria have certainly not been ones I normally consider. However, I expect there are and will be some prospects who would meet your needs."

"Any help you can provide would be greatly appreciated," Mace said, rising.

"I am impressed that you would seek me out for this, Marshal."

"I thought it only made sense. Thank you for your time."

"My pleasure, Marshal," she said, rising and going with him to the front door.

* * *

The deaths of telegraph operator Authur Lundy and Amadahy, the seventeen-year-old wife of Esau Falzon, was sent singing up and down the telegraph wires from Pryor Creek. The next day, Falzon returned from Gibson Station. He had to suppress his glee. Everything had worked out just as planned. However, the businessman forced himself not to smile as the train stopped, and he disembarked.

Falzon bumped into a man in a sweat-stained hat wearing a tan corduroy jacket. Falzon's expression instantly changed to one of offense as he glared at the man who was now holding Falzon's .36 caliber revolver which belonged in Falzon's shoulder holster.

"I beg your pardon!" Falzon said, meaning no such apology.

"You Esau Falzon?"

"I am — and that is my pistol you have just lifted from me."

"You won't be needing it," said Heck Thomas.

"Why is that?"

The man pulled his coat aside to reveal a Deputy U.S. Marshal's badge. "You are under arrest for the attempted murder of your wife, Amadahy, and Authur Lundy."

"Attempted?" Falzon asked, amazed.

"They didn't die," Deputy Marshal Thomas said, turning Falzon around and clamping handcuffs on him.

Falzon was dazed when he saw his wife and the telegraph operator step out of the train station alive and well.

When Thomas turned Falzon back around, the Marshal explained, "I put some of your 'sleeping powder' in a bowl of water outside Dr. Gowicki's office. The good doctor had noticed the almond smell of the power Mr. Lundy brought him in the little envelope you gave him. The doctor and I had shared breakfast a few hours before, and he knew I was in town. We devised a test of just a portion of your powder.

"This morning, we found two dead rats, a stray cat, and the body of a raccoon near the bowl. Cyanide."

Heck Thomas moved the would-be killer off the platform with a shove.

"She's still my wife?" he bellowed.

"She won't be after you hang," Thomas told him.

# CHAPTER 14

E ach time Claxton Landers returned to <u>The Ledger</u>, something was always changed. Most times, he couldn't put a finger on it, but eventually, he realized that all the clutter and dust he was so used to working with had disappeared. His supplies, bottles of ink, rollers, cans of solvent were wiped down and lined up orderly.

Since Mena Vickery had started to work as the paper's copy editor, obituary, and advertisement writer, as well as receptionist, her natural smile and wit had made everyone who entered feel welcome. To Claxton, the attractive woman made the office a place not of just creativity and work but of fun and joy. She kept a pot of coffee on the ready all day long. Often Mena was at the office before Claxton climbed out of bed.

She had also changed him without saying a word. He shaved every day, wore a clean shirt, and saw to his overall appearance in ways he'd not done in years.

"Now that we have three pages each issue," he began one day as he was setting type, " — because of your ad sales," he said, "I need more copy to fill it. Any suggestions?"

"Have you ever considered that about half your readers are of the female persuasion?" she asked, checking over the latest article Claxton had completed and printed as a galley sheet.

"No. So?"

"The wives, sisters, and mothers of every household have more to say about what comes in and out of the home than do the men." She looked up at him with a grin, "Believe it or not."

"Oh, I don't doubt it. I know my father was the head of our home, but it was Mother who had the last word."

"Such being the case," she said, turning back to the galley proof, "what do you include in The Ledger to appeal to women?"

"I never considered such a thing," Claxton said, rubbing his chin with ink-stained fingers.

Mena glanced at him and stroked her own chin.

"Huh?" he asked.

"Ink."

Claxton looked down at his hands and reached for a rag and some solvent. "What do you suggest? What do women want?"

"How about recipes?"

"What recipes?"

"We could request ladies to submit their favorite? Print one in each issue."

"That's a good idea."

She motioned for him to come to her with her fingers. He stepped across the office to her desk, and she took the damp rag from him. She dapped a couple of spots he had missed on his chin. When finished, she returned the cloth.

The touch of her finger, even through the rag, sent a ripple through Claxton. What was he feeling?

She went back to her work as if unaware of what had just happened.

"And, how about a lovelorn column?"

It took a moment before Claxton could put words together again. He capped the can of solvent and draped the rag to air out and dry.

"Lovelorn?"

"Let's call it an advice column. A kind of 'Dear Aunt Phoebe' where people could ask questions — like, when should I let him kiss me for the first time — or I'm widowed and want to know when it is proper for me to flirt with a man again? That kind of thing."

"Who would write it?"

"I could," Mena said, holding out Claxton's marked up galley proof. "It wouldn't be that hard."

"But you're doing so much now."

"When you're not here, there are hours I sit around with not a thing to do."

"Except to clean, dust, and polish."

"You did notice?" she laughed.

"How could I not. This place has never looked so good."

"Well, thank you," Mena said. "Think about a recipe and an advice column. I'll bet they would both be popular.

Claxton set to work adding the name Mrs. Mena Vickery — Copy Editor to the papers copywrite and credit block.

"You need to think up a pseudonym," he said, "— so no one will know who is writing the advice."

* * *

After the death of Belle's husband, Weaver Reed, by a deputy sheriff near Paris, Texas, she had to decide what to do next with herself and her family.

Even though Belle's father, John Shirly, had accepted his daughter and her two children back into the family in Texas, even while Weaver Reed was still on the run, it was now time for her to move on.

Belle wanted to return to Missouri. But there was a better hideout she had learned about called Younger Bend. It was in the Cherokee portion of The Indian Territory. This hideout was the result of years of division within the Cherokee people.

The Cherokee nation had long been split between two political factions. One, the Ross faction, was made up mostly of the descendents of the marriages between Scottish men and Cherokee women. John Ross, one of their number, rose in Cherokee politics to represent the tribe in Washington, D.C. Ross later became tribal Chief. He was a leader against the removal of the Cherokee to The Nations —

however, the U.S. Government ultimately prevailed, and the *"trail of tears"* to the Indian Territory was the result.

The Ross faction evolved into the Starr faction after Ross died. They were troublemakers and outlaws. Tom Starr was their new leader. The Cherokee tribal government was so frustrated with Starr and his band that they made a special treaty with him. In it, Starr and his gang were given amnesty, a share of the tribal treasury and land of their own. For his part, Starr promised to behave himself and his men within the Cherokee land. This land was a remote stretch between Brairtown and Eufaula on a bend of the Canadian River in the Hi-Early mountains. They called it Younger's Bend after the Younger brothers who had frequently stayed with the Starrs and were spending the rest of their lives in prison.

Once, visiting her then-husband Weaver Reed, Belle met Uriah Starr, one of Tom's sons. The handsome and virile Uriah was a moonshiner and horse thief. So it was that after Weaver's death, Belle fled to Younger's Bend.

She dressed as a man and won respect from others with her horsemanship and her ability with firearms. Belle accompanied other bandits to rob wealthy Creeks who had their section of the Indian Territory.

The widow Reed sent her son to live with the mother of her former husband, Weaver. Her daughter, Pearl, Belle then sent to boarding schools in Arkansas. She put her full attention to the life she wanted, rustling horses and cattle running whiskey to Indians, burglarizing stores, and even hijacked tribal treasures.

She married Uriah Starr and thus had access to his share of tribal lands.

Belle soon came to dominate the gang. While she rarely participated in any of the raids, she was the planning and the brains behind the bandits. Belle galvanized her gang by securing them legal representation, bail, and reduced sentences if not dropped charges. Still, she loved the excitement of the outlaw life and just couldn't help herself.

Her big mistake came when Deputy Marshal Cornelius Carney arrested Belle for a second time on horse-stealing charges. Judge

Parker had freed her the last time she stood before him of the same charge. It was different this time.

Carney had stopped Belle and Uriah together, leading the stolen horse and arrested the pair on the spot. They were going back into court with a much stronger case against them this time.

# CHAPTER 15

Fifteen-year-old cowboy and former slave, Ford Telton, came into Ft. Smith, with his legs dangling off the back of a weather-worn farm wagon. It was undignified, but the boy was so tired he had held onto the side of the wagon and struggled to stay awake.

A cowboy without a horse, the saying goes, is afoot. His horse had run away from him, frightened by an approaching prairie fire. The roaring blaze set by a band of attacking Indians who had raided the small herd of cattle Telton was helping move from Texas to Sedalia, Missouri. He got himself wet in the creek and huddled down under the lip of the gully as the inferno raced up and over.

From there, the young man had walked from the eastern Indian Territory to Dallas, Arkansas, in Polk County. He soon learned that if he were going to get any action on his story of the Indian attack on the Hence and Adell Blevin's cattle drive, he needed to go up to Ft. Smith.

The wagon stopped, and Ford Telton shook himself fully awake.

"We're at the courthouse, boy," the older man driving the wagon said. "You'll find the Marshal in his office upstairs."

Telton wobbled a moment as he jumped down but quickly gained his balance.

"Thank you, sir," he said, tipping his battered hat.

"Glad t' help. Good luck."

The wagon drove off.

Telton found the outside stairs and a sign with a badge on it and an arrow pointing up.

Mace was in his office, pinning a badge on a newly sworn-in Deputy Marshal. He heard the slow footsteps coming up the stairs. Mace shook hands with the new Deputy who took three warrants off of Mace's desk and left.

The Marshal was about to sit down behind his desk when the young black cowboy appeared at this door. The teen removed his hat.

"Marshal?" he asked.

"Yes. Come in."

"I'm Ford Telton."

"Marshal Mace Truax. What can I do for you?"

The cowboy started to tell his tale but slumped to his knees before he could get to the meat of his story.

"When was the last time you ate?" Mace asked.

The boy had to take a couple of breaths before he could say a day or two ago. I ain't sure, Marshal."

Mace was up and lifted the young man off the floor.

"Then you come with me. Let's get a good meal in you."

"Bless you, sir."

* * *

Mace took the young man to Ma Nauman's Cafe, a block from the courthouse. He ordered the boy two steaks, potatoes, fresh bread, peach pie, and all the milk Telton could hold. The Marshal watched in amazement at the amount of food the cowboy could consume.

When the boy finally sat back, he burped before he could get his hand to cover his mouth. Mace smiled and clapped him on the back.

"Anything else," a waitress asked, refilling Tilton's glass with milk.

"Coffee?" Mace asked, and the kid nodded his head.

The cowboy finished the milk before the waitress returned with a pot of coffee and two cups.

"Now," Mace said, "you were telling me about a cattle drive up from Texas?"

"Yes, sir. Mr. Hence Blevin and his bride, Miss Adell, was taking a herd of 'bout three hundred head up the Shawnee Trail. There was four hands. They and th' Blevins were all asleep. I was riding night hawk when the Indians hit."

"How many warriors?"

"I reckon five — may' b seven or eight. They rode right into camp and shot or clubbed everybody. I knows the Blevins, and ever one else is dead when the shootin' stopped. The cattle jumped up and started to stampede. I turned coward an' ran away."

"I doubt you could have done anything by yourself," Mace told the boy. "If you hadn't left, who would have come here with the story?"

"I guess," the cowboy said. "But, I still feel ashamed."

"Don't. There was nothin' you could have done — except what you have."

"Well, they must' a knowed about me cause they started a prairie fire with the wind blowin' the way I was ridin'. I finds this little creek down in a gully, and that's when my hoss jumped away from me and ran. I think she must have smelled the fire, 'for I seen it. All I could do was t' get myself wet as I could and hunker down. The fire swept over me, and 'bout took all the air with it. I thought I'd never get my breath. But finally, I did."

The young man paused before he went on. "That's when I started walkin' toward Arkansas. I got t' a town called Dallas, and they told me I'd need to come up here and see the Marshal or no one would ever go after them Indians."

"Did you know what tribe they were?"

"No, sir."

"Could you identify any of those you saw if you ever saw them again?"

"I could, and I would — on my momma's soul, I would."

\* \* \*

Mace was called into Judge Parker's off at the end of court one day.

"Have you had a chance to meet Deputy Marshal Nim Defert," the Judge asked, handing Mace a letter with nine signatures on it.

"Irish, short, sure of himself but not belligerent — doesn't drink to excess — doesn't gamble. He's liked by most but a hard man when he has to be. I spent most of a day with him last time he was in." Mace slapped the letter with the back of his hand. "He's not this man."

"What about Rush Creek?"

"It's on the Washita. In southern part of Chickasaw country. It's notorious as the best of times."

"I'd like to see Defert next time he's in," Judge Parker said.

"So would I. Could we meet him together, Your Honor."

"Excellent idea, Marshal."

"I'll let you know, Judge."

# CHAPTER 16

Within a couple of weeks, Sebastian County had a new sheriff. Scrawny thirty-five-year-old Whitney Tatterman was appointed Sheriff of Sabastian, Arkansas. Greenwood was the county seat, but the Sheriff's Office was located in Ft. Smith. Tatterman dressed in a subtle plaid suit and bowler hat. He had thick mutton chops down his cheeks but was bald when he removed his hat. The shiny badge on his chest couldn't make up for the fact that Tatterman was first and last a politician, not a lawman. This job was a path to more prominent and more significant offices.

He hired four tough and intimidating deputies. They were not men Mace would have ever put Deputy Marshal badges on but they were the new Sheriff's choices. Tatterman dressed his me in khaki shirts and pants, with new black hats. They had deputy badges and wore cross-draw Peacemaker Colts.

The long-closed cells in the Sheriff's office were quickly doing a steady, often overnight business. The new visibility of the deputies and the commonly seen figure of Tatterman resulted in a more orderly and law-abiding town and county.

\* \* \*

Mace was having a beer in The Sidewheeler when a man in his midforties approached. He looked to be dressed in new jeans, shirt and vest. He also looked shaved and had his hair cut recently.

"Marshal Truax?" the man asked.

"Yes," Mace answered.

"I am Bezzle. Buz Bezzle. I'm a rancher from Texas."

"Mr. Bezzle, won't you join me for a beer?'

"It'd be a pleasure, Marshal."

Bezzle was a man of the outdoors. His deeply tanned skin testified to this as did his broad chest and muscular arms.

Mace signaled Jules Morgan, co-owner bartender, to bring two beers.

"I sold a herd up in Sedalia, and I'm on my way back t' Texas. But I saw your ad in several newspapers I've read. You still looking for deputies?"

"Yes."

Jules set a cold beer in front of each man. Mace gave the bartender two bits.

"What I noticed in your ad," Bezzle continued after his first drink, "was you didn't say 'no Mexicans and no darkies.'"

"I'm looking for men who can do the job, Mr. Bezzle."

"That's what I was hoping to hear." The rancher took a drink. "I've got this ramrod who I think might fit your bill. He's good with his hands, his gun — and can handle men."

"I'd like to meet him," Mace said.

"Good, after we finish this beer I'll take you to him."

* * *

"Again, Mrs. Starr," Judge Parker said after the charges were read against her and her husband. Belle had no answer. She sat in her chair beside Uriah and waited while Temple Houston rose.

"Your honor, my clients, Mr. and Mrs. Starr, are here because of an ongoing grievance between them and Deputy Marshal Cornelius Carney. Since the last time Deputy Carney attempted to have Mrs.

Starr sent to prison, he has been hiding out and stalking them. In this case, they were merely borrowing a horse from a neighbor."

"A neighbor outside the Cherokee portion of The Nations, as I understand it," Judge Parker said. "And a neighbor over forty miles away."

"Sometimes, one's neighbors are nowhere near in this land, Your Honor."

"Does the Prosecution have the 'neighbor' to call as a witness?"

"I do, Your Honor. Mr. Charley Tal Loaf."

"Call your first witness, Mr. Dalby," Judge Parker said.

Carley Tal Loaf, a strong, stocky man with a broad face and dark eyes, took the stand after he was sworn in.

"Mr. Tal Loaf," Rupert Dalby began, "do you consider yourself a neighbor of Mr. and Mrs. Starr?"

"No. I have never seen them before today."

"So you did not loan them the use of your sixteen hands tall, dun Belgian Draft horse?"

"No. I do not loan my horses unless I am with them."

"Are you sure the horse in question, the one Deputy Marshal Carney is holding in a local livery, is your horse?"

"I am."

"No further questions, Your Honor."

Temple Houston stood and crossed to the witness.

"One brown draft horse looks pretty much like another. How can you be positive his one is yours?"

"She has my brand."

"We all know brands can be changed, Mr. Tal Loaf."

"But she also has a scar on her left flank where she was cut as a colt. She is my horse. No doubt."

Temple thought and walked back to his table. He eyed his clients and finally sighed and shook his head, saying, "No more questions."

"The witness may step down," Judge Parker said.

When Deputy Marshal Cornelius Carney took the stand, the thirty-seven-year-old with a red mustache, which hung below his jawline, sat with his Montana Peak hat in his lap.

"Marshal Carney, when did you arrest the defendants?" Dalby asked.

"About a minute after they knocked down Mr. Tal Loaf's fence and led his horse onto the road."

"Had you been watching them?"

"For about a week. I knew they'd pull something like this sooner or later. And I caught'em red-handed."

"Any question in your mind about the identity of this couple or the stolen horse.

"Not a single one," Carney said.

There simply wasn't much Temple Houston could to or say. The jury deliberated only five minutes and returned with a verdict of guilty.

Judge Parker had the couple stand. Temple stood with them. The Judge said, "Having been found guilty of horse theft by a jury of your peers, I now sentence each of you to nine months in the Detroit Federal House of Correction in Michigan."

Judge Parker rapped his gavel and ended court for the day.

# CHAPTER 17

A new warrant in hand, Deputy Marshal Jacob Yost and his posse of fifteen were determined to apprehend Cherokee outlaw Ned Christi. The one-thousand-dollar reward for Christi, dead or alive, had added five bounty hunters to the group. The ten Marshals had borrowed a small Army cannon and two mules to haul it. They brought plenty of ammunition and even boxes of dynamite.

Ned Christi's castle, as some had labeled it, was also known as the "*Rabbit Trap*." It was in Wauhillau, about a dozen miles from Stillwell. In the five years the full-blooded Cherokee, and member of the Executive Tribal Council, had been wanted, he had built himself a fortress. Both a gunsmith and blacksmith himself, Christi enlisted the help of friends and neighbors to build his fortress. The outpost was a fortified wall around a cabin inside the defensive wall. The walls of both the fort and the cabin were double-walled. The space between the walls was filled with rocks and sand. The location had a wide killing field in front of it, and any approaching riders could be seen miles away.

Christi was initially wanted in connection with the death of U.S. Deputy Marshal Dan Maples. Maples was hunting illegal alcohol sellers when he was gunned down from ambush. Because Christi was known to have been sleeping off the effect of some whiskey he had purchased, he was one of the original suspects in the Marshal's murder.

All other suspects were apprehended, questioned, and released -- all except for Ned Christi. The staunch supporter for tribal rights and sovereignty, Christi was soon the only remaining possibility. The Cherokee always claimed his innocence and did not trust his fate to the white man's court in Ft. Smith. He did, however, write a couple of letters to Judge Parker expressing his position and asking for time to investigate the matter and discover who the actual killer was. The Judge ignored all these letters.

Deputy Marshal Jacob Yost was lanky, six feet tall, robust, and unyielding. At thirty, Yost had been a sheriff in Abilene, Kansas. He had a short red beard, deep-set blue eyes, a high forehead. He commanded his posse, and no one questioned his authority or directions.

When the band of lawmen and bounty hunters arrived at Ned Christi's castle, they took cover behind boulders and trees. Yost quickly grasped the situation and how well Christi was defended. He called out for Christi to surrender or be attacked.

The Cherokee's answer was a simple, "No!"

Yost spread his men out, and they began a siege while the cannon was brought up and positioned. The shells from the artillery piece did little damage because of the range and the nature of the fortifications. The charge in the cannon was double, but this only resulted in the cracking of the cannon barrel. For two days, the posse pounded away at the fortress with little result. Sticks of dynamite were thrown but did not reach the walls before they exploded. One of the bounty hunters was wounded, and two Deputy Marshals suffered cuts from shattered rocks and tree bark.

"The only way we're going to get in there," Yost told his men the second night, "is to blast and burn him out."

"How we going to do that?" another Marshal asked.

"I think we'll take the cannon off its wheels and load the carriage up with wood and straw. We'll concentrate our fire from over on the right while a five men set the thing on fire and shove it up against the wall. Once they're that near, I want dynamite tossed against the wall and over it."

The plan was carried out the next day. It took several hours during the night to reposition the cannon's wheel mounts. Then beginning at first light, a blistering gunfire barrage was unloaded on the castle while the carriage set ablaze and rammed up against the wooden fortification walls.

The fire caught the log structure, but it didn't get past the first wall. Most of the rocks and sand remained. The dynamite did more damage.

A surprise came when a call came from the fortress to allow the women and children to leave.

Marshal Yost agreed to the request and had a party of six officers checked those who reluctantly exited the barricade. They were all women and children. They were kept together and not allowed to leave the area for fear they might sound an alarm and seek neighbors to come join the fight.

Once all the noncombatants were out, the fight renewed.

Torches and more dynamite sticks were thrown over the walls. Holes were opened in the smoldering bulwark, and the cabin caught fire. Finally, late that third day, when Yost called for a cease-fire from his party, it was noted that no gunfire was coming from the castle. Few at a time, the members of the posse made their way to the chared walls and gates.

When the full compliment stormed through the gate, Ned Christi was found dead along with three companions. The posse throughly searched the whole position and found no other fighters. The women and children were allowed to return.

Despite the wailing and the death cries, Yost secured Ned Christi's body, and the posse returned to Stillwell. There Christi's body was laid out on an unattached door, propped up, and a picture taken with some of the Marshals. Christi's Henry rifle was placed in his cold hands for the image.

Christi's body was shipped back to Ft. Smith, and the case was closed. Then, after all the newspaper and magazine coverage of the affair, a white witness, Dick Humphreys, an Irishman who had been traveling through Stillwell, came forward. He sent a letter to Judge Parker from Texas. Humphreys said he saw the shooting but was threatened by the real killer, Bud Trainer.

Trainer, a notorious gunrunner, and whiskey maker, had been one of the original suspects but was cleared because of lack of evidence. Trainer threatened Humphreys, who continued on his way to Texas.

Trainer had been killed days before the siege on Ned Christi. A whiskey deal gone bad had resulted in Trainer's death by two shotguns.

Christi was buried near his home and was always thought to be an outlaw regardless of facts.

# CHAPTER 18

The Range was a bar that appealed to blacks and Hispanic cowboys. It was a loud place with sawdust on the floors and a mariachi band featuring a trumpet blaring. A colorful and shapely young woman danced with castanets, stomping feet, and whirling skirts. Rancher and trailboss Buz Bezzle came with Mace to look for a man Bezzle throught would make a good deputy for the Marshal. The man they were looking for leaned against the back wall. He was tall with dark eyes that missed nothing. He wore a cowboy hat, vest, and Vacarro pants, split over his boots. His hatband, his vest, and down the outer seam of his pants were all studded with shiny conchos.

Raul Vega smiled when his boss approach. After trying to talk, Bezzle motioned to the outside, and all three left the bar.

Bezzle introduced Mace to Vega two buildings down the street. The two men shook hands. Vega leaned against a hitching rail.

"Raul did a great job helping get the herd up the trail. But I don't think the cowboy life is for him. He's a good man, honest, and dependable. I've been thinking about him as a deputy marshal ever since I read your first ad, Marshal. Raul?"

"Señor Bezzle is too kind," Vega said with only a hint of Spanish accent. "I did the job I was hired to do."

The rancher described the reason for the meeting, and Vega stuck out his bottom lip in thought. "I've never thought about being a lawman."

"It's a tough job. We work for Judge Parker's court and mostly in the Indian Territory. We have warrants for killers, robbers, gun, and whiskey runners. Our job is to arrest and bring outlaws in to stand trial. Sometimes it involves using your gun, sometimes not. We also work with the tribal Indian Police. They, too, have authority all over the seventy-square miles of the Territory. The crimes we're interested in are federal crimes — crimes by whites, or blacks, or Mexicans against Indians. Or crimes of Indians against whites, blacks, or Mexicans."

Vega said nothing for a few moments then slowly began to nod his head.

"Do you speak any Indian languages?" Mace asked.

"Very little."

"Well, your Spanish would be beneficial. Many of the tribes, especially those near Mexico, do speak Spanish. Several of the plains tribes do too — or they at least understand it."

Again Vega nodded his head.

"My office is upstairs in the courthouse. See me tomorrow morning, and we'll get you sworn in. There's a warrant I have for some Indians who killed a young couple with a small herd. The renegades murdered the couple and three other cowboys. Then the Indians stole the cattle. I've been waiting for an Indian Policeman to return from another job. He's back now. He'd be a good man to pair you up with. His name is Browneagle. He taught me the ropes of what Deputy Marshals are up against out there. I think he can do the same for you."

"Thank you, Señor Bezzle. It was a pleasure working for you."

"You're welcome, my friend," the rancher said.

"Marshal, I will come to your office, mañana."

Mace shook hands with Vega and left Bezzle to do some celebrating with his former ramrod.

* * *

The next day Mace sent Raul Vega, and John Browneagle together from Ft. Smith looking for War Dog — a renegade whom Browneagle knew. Young Ford Telton, the only surviving trail hand of the ill-fated drive, had taken the job at Howell Keeling Mercantile unloading wagons and restocking merchandise. He promised to stay in town until there was a trial.

The Marshal had lunch that day with Delta Wadsworth at The Craig House, the best formal dining place in Ft. Smith .

Mace looked up to a see dusty, trail worn man who approach the table. The man wore a Deputy Marshal's badge on his faded and shabby plaid shirt. He also carried a pistol slung low on his left hip.

"Marshal Truax?" he asked as he stepped up to the table Mace was sharing with Delta.

"I'm Deputy Nim Defert. Just brought in a wagon load of prisoners. Over at the jail, I was told you wanted t' see me. Stonewall Welch told me where I might find you."

Mace got to his feet and offered his hand, but the man, after at first reciprocating, pulled his back.

"You and the lady," he said, tipping his hat, "are eating, Marshal. I'm 'bout as dirty as a buffalo fresh out of a waller."

Mace smiled and dropped his hand.

"I'm glad to meet you, Deputy Defert. This is Mrs. Delta Wadsworth."

"Ma'am," Defert said. Delta was wearing her dark brown hair down in curls to her shoulders. The Deputy noticed how lovely the Marshal's companion was

"Actually, it's Judge Parker who wants to see us both," Mace said. "And it's not in that big a rush. How about around four this afternoon in the Judge's office. He usually takes a break about that time between cases."

"That would fine with me, Marshal," the five foot eight inch Irishman said. "Give me a chance to cut some of this fur off me," he said, stroking his scruffy face, "and ma'be get a new shirt."

"Then, I'll see you upstairs at the courthouse around four."

"I'll be there, Marshal." Defert tipped his hand again, "Ma'am, sorry for disturbing your lunch."

"Not at all, Deputy," Delta said.

Mace retook his seat and picked up his fork before saying, "You were saying?"

"Your sister got a raise."

"At the paper? She's only been working there a month or so."

"But The Ledger is doing much better. Have you noticed it has added a third page?"

"That I see."

"How about the new columns — recipes and Ask Aunt Hildegarde?"

Mace laughed. "Oh, yes. Not that I read them."

"You should."

"Why?"

"Your sister is Aunt Hildegarde. Keep that to yourself. There are only a very few people who know."

"Really? I wouldn't have imagined. Is she also writing the recipes?"

"No. Readers submit them. Mena tries them out on her girls — and me, since I'm a frequent guest — and even you? Remember that dutch apple pie she served last Sunday?"

"That *was* good."

"It was in today's paper."

"My sister, a newspaper writer."

"What is that meeting with Judge Parker, the Deputy, and you all about?"

"There's a petition demanding that Defert be fired."

"For what?"

"Misconduct. We'll see in a couple of hours."

# CHAPTER 19

The trial of Esau Falzon took only a couple of hours at the start of court one day. Falzon had attempted to poison his Cherokee wife, Amadahy, and the man who was caring for her, telegraph operator Authur Lundy.

Falzon pleaded innocent to the charges. The testimony of a local physician, Dr. Gowicki, and Deputy Marshal Heck Thomas to the death of small animals who drank from a water bowl containing some of the *"sleeping powder"* Falzon had left for his wife proved the concoction was deadly. A Ft. Smith pharmacist supported that testimony saying he had tested the powder, and it was over fifty percent cyanide.

His attorney tried to persuade the jury that the deadly mixture was not what Falzon had left with Authur Lundy for his wife. However, two other merchants from Pryor Creek told of Falzon's mistreatment of his wife. One offered the opinion that the only reason Falzon married Amadahy was to obtain rights to Cherokee tribal land.

The jury brought back a verdict of guilty after only fifteen minutes, and Judge Parker sentenced Falzon to hang.

\* \* \*

That same afternoon Judge Parker moved to the case of Emery Haguse. The charge against the soft, round-faced man with a nervous twitch of his left eye was the murder of a traveling school teacher. Wilber Gabel, the dead man, was supposedly a friend of Haguse. But after the body of the young teacher was found hung up on a tree branch in a creek, a bullet hole was discovered his back and his recently paid yearly salary was missing.

Like many before him, Emery Haguse's claimed he was innocent of the charge against him. What he could not explain was the exact amount of cash Wilber Gabel had been issued three days earlier, minus only two dollars. And Haguse had no job or source of income.

The final nail in his case was the monogrammed concho Haguse was carrying in his pocket when arrested. This was an item made for Wilber Gabel by some of his students.

Haguse did not take the stand but blubbered at the defense table as the jury filed out. The verdict of guilty didn't take but five minutes this time. Again, like other killers before him, Judge Parker sentenced to hang.

* * *

From his jail cell under the courthouse, Esau Falzon called another lawyer, Temple Houston, to draft a will.

"I want to cut her out of everything," the smoldering Falzon told Houston. "When I die, I don't want her to get one wooden nickel."

"From what you've told me, Mr. Falzon, the land both your stores sit on is not your land but Cherokee land. You have no legal right to dispose of it. At your death, it will all pass to your wife."

"Then, I want to divorce her!" Falzon shouted.

The other prisoners in the cell looked around at Falzon huddled in one corner with the fancy-dressed lawyer.

"On what grounds?" Houston asked.

"Adultery. She was living with Authur Lundy. Everybody in town knew it."

"All right. That I can do," Houston said. "I'll draft a divorce petition this afternoon and submit it to Judge Parker."

"Is that all that's needed?"

"Not quite. I'll need to get statements from people in Pryor Creek that she was committing adultery by living with Authur Lundy."

"That shouldn't be hard."

"No, I expect it will take about a week or so. However, I can't submit the petition until I have those sworn statements."

"Then what?"

"Then it's up to Judge Parker."

"What can he do?"

"The Judge has a full slate of cases and legal matters already on his desk. It's simply a matter of his accepting the petition and acting on it."

"How long are we talking about?"

"That's the thing, Mr. Falzon — Judge Parker is trying to get through a two-year backlog of cases and petitions as quickly as he can."

"Meaning — what?" Falzon asked suspiciously.

"There's no way of knowing when he will get to this matter. Perhaps a month — perhaps two months or more."

"You're telling me he might not act on this until after I'm hung?"

"A genuine possibility, I'm sorry to tell you."

Falzon's face turned pale as he sank to the floor in despair.

* * *

Judge Parker called the Snee trial to order. Eben Snee, the half Cherokee, and half German-American was accused of the murder of Mr. And Mrs. Stilegebouer, a farming couple, and the hiding of their bodies.

District Attorney Rupert Dalby rose and made his opening statement.

In part, he said, "The Prosecution will prove that this man," he pointed a knotty finger at the skinny but rock hard defendant, "murdered the Stilegebouers with no need or reason. He killed without mercy, and then hid their bodies, expecting no one ever to find them. You will see parts of their bodies recovered by our lawmen. This man is the kind the law was created to deal with — and you gentlemen of the jury will have that task — to find him guilty of this murder he has confessed to and of which we will produce evidence of commission."

Snee's court-appointed attorney, Gilderoy Cheatham, stooped shouldered, with curly red hair, and a beard that covered his jawline, stood to speak.

"I wager every one of you men in the jury have — at one or more times in your life — gotten falling down drunk and did things you very much regretted the next day. That is my client. The confession he wrote was even made while he was under the influence of the evil spirit rum. Regardless of the evidence you hear, I would like for you to keep in mind that these things were done while Mr. Snee was not in his right mind. Drink had deprived him of reason and even common sense. You have been there. What if it were you sitting there days or even weeks after you had been on a bender? You might be guilty — but your actions were those of the devil — not of a rational man."

The testimony of Sheriff Glover Barrows established the cruel and vicious nature of Eben Snee, even on his best days. The Sheriff also swore to the signed confession Snee had signed in the Sheriff's jail.

From Deputy Marshal Cornelius Carney and Lighthorse Policeman John Browneagle, the scene at the Stilegebouer farm was painted. The petty theft of canned foods suggested the only reason for the murders. All three lawmen told the tale of recovering the bodies from the mountain fissure.

This jury needed less than a quarter-hour to review the evidence and find Snee guilty of vicious murders. According to the law, Judge Parker sentenced Snee to hang by his neck until he was dead.

# CHAPTER 20

The grass was already sprouting through the blackened earth where the prairie fire had raged. Browneagle and newly minted Deputy Marshal Raul Vega followed the scorched ground back to where it had been set ablaze.

As they examined what remained of the chared chuck wagon and the campsite, Browneagle found where young Hence Blevin had been cooked above the coals of his own campfire Stretched across the circle of stones lay the man's scorched bones and his ashes.

At the wagon, the dark eyes of Raul Vega found the remains of another body.

"The wife," Browneagle explained. "Wider hips than the man. They raped her at the end of the wagon."

"Was she dead or alive?" Vega asked.

"War Dog and his men would have rather her be alive — but it wouldn't matter to them."

The Deputy found the remains of a shovel and dug two graves. Browneagle cut his blanket in half to hold each skeleton.

Back in the saddle, they rode until the prairie fire marks played out. There they picked up the marks left by the cattle. The two followed those marks to a trading post where the owner confirmed he had bought cattle from War Dog and eight braves. The man didn't know if they were stolen or not — but he said he wouldn't live long in his business if he asked too many questions.

For the next few days, Browneagle and Vega searched the country-side and questioned everyone they came across. They continued to be drawn further Northwest. It was suspected by all they talked with that a band of renegades lead by War Dog had a camp somewhere in the foothills.

The late fall heat was upon the lawmen as they searched and tracked the Indian band. They discovered the renegade camp but pulled away and talked as they checked their weapons.

"They're drinking," Browneagle said. "A couple of hours and we can take them all."

"I didn't see any lookout?"

"They don't think anybody would dare approach them."

"They're going to be in for *mucho* surprise."

* * *

In the foothills where the renegade Indian gang drank and danced. Lighthorse Policeman John Browneagle and Deputy Marshal Raul Vega readied themselves to move into the savage's camp. Yet, before either could make a move, a fight broke out between two of the nine wild and uncivilized men.

The two swiped at each other with their blades, and each suffered cuts. Anger and whiskey drove the two on until one lunged and stabbed his opponent in the stomach. However, as the wounded man fell forward, he had enough strength to bury his knife in his killer's back. Both men dropped to the dirt bleeding and taking only a few more breaths.

From around the fire, three other warriors staggered to their feet and stumbled over to check the two bodies. In their language, they reported to the rest that both men in the dirt were dead. One of the trio poured some of his whiskey on his fallen companions. This made all the men laugh and drink again.

On that note, Browneagle and Vega got to their feet, both chambering a round into their rifles as they stepped into the light. In Choctaw, Browneagle shouted for them to not move.

The group looked up but were unable to fully grasp what was happening. One brave, grabbed his rifle, and Vega cut him down before the man could even get the weapon up into firing position. Another tried the same thing, and Browneagle shot him.

The remaining five were sobering up as they got awkwardly to their feet. Their leader, War Dog, said something in Choctaw to Browneagle.

"The cattle you stole — the man and his wife you killed — as well as the other cowboys," the Lighthorse Policeman said in English.

War Dog stepped forward, slapping himself on the chest.

"War Dog killed the man — I cooked him over his own fire! I also shot the woman! Anyone else," he said to the others in his group, "who says he did it, lies!"

"I kill one," the youngest, Bear Killer, of the group declared.

"Me kill two others," another said.

One of the warriors who couldn't claim a killing as his own pulled his knife and turned on Deputy Vega. Raul shot the drunk Indian before he could take a single step.

And then there were only four left.

"Put handcuffs on them," Browneagle said to Vega.

The lawman stepped back and grabbed two pairs of cuffs from behind the rock where he had been hiding. He secured War Dog and the warrior nearest him. Vega shoved both of them to their knees.

The Deputy went to where Browneagle had been waiting and picked up the two pairs of cuffs he brought. Vega cuffed the remaining two.

While those now under arrest waited, Browneagle loaded the bodies on their horses and knotted all their bridles together. Lastly, Vega covered those on the ground while the Indian Policeman took the prisoners one by one and tied them to their horses.

\* \* \*

John Browneagle and Raul Vega rode into Durant, a Choctaw town in the southern part of the tribe's land. Indian Policeman Browneagle led four horses with the arrested remains of War Dog's renegade gang down the main street. Deputy Vega had five horses trailing him with the bodies of the dead gang members. The live prisoners sat defiantly on their horses, their legs tied under their mounts. Only Bear Killer, the youngest of the four, hung his head in shame. War Dog cursed him demanded that he act like a man.

The Choctaw was one of the *"Five Civilized Tribes."* Originally they were from what became Alabama, Florida, Mississippi, and Lousiana. As a people, the Choctaw consolidated in the 1600s and developed three distinct political and geographical divisions — eastern, western and southern. They had helped and supported the Thirteen Original Colonies during the American Revolution. In fact, the Choctaw never went to war against the United States. And yet they were betrayed and forcibly relocated in 1831-1833, under the Indian Removal act. First moved in two groups, one to land along the Mississippi and the other into the Indian Territory. Finally, even those in Mississippi were forced to join their brothers and sisters in The Nations.

The sheriff of Durant was a Choctaw. The people of the town gathered around the mounted group as Browneagle talked to the sheriff. The people were ashamed and disgusted with War Dog and his men. The sheriff agreed to take the bodies of the dead and see that the death rights were performed for them. The four left alive were led away with Browneagle and Vega for Ft. Smith.

* * *

Mace and Deputy Defert waited outside the Judge's office when the jurist came up the stairs from the courtroom below.

"This is Deputy Nim Defert. He arrived a few hours ago."

"Deputy," Judge Parker offered his hand to the thirty-year-old man. They shook hands, and the Judge opened his office door. Mace and Defert followed.

Parker stayed on his feet after he hung up his robe. He found the petition under a stack of paper on his desk and handed it across to Defert.

"Do you read, Deputy?"

"Yes, sir."

The Judge and Mace stood while Defert read the document. Mace noticed that the Deputy had a new shirt and jeans on. He'd shaved and had a haircut.

Defert shook his head and opened his mouth in surprise. When he looked up, the Deputy said, "Your Honor, four of the names on this are now in jail right below us. The others — they're crooks in one way or another. I wouldn't be surprised to be picking up warrants for any of them before I head out again."

Defert handed Judge Parker back the paper.

"Thank you, Deputy. I wanted to hear that from you before I file this," the Judge said as he wadded the sheet up and dropped it into a trash can beside his desk. "Mace?"

"I agree, Your Honor."

"Then let's not spend any more time on this. Good afternoon."

"Judge," Defert nodded, and Mace followed him out the door.

Out in the hall, Mace asked, "Can I buy you a beer, Deputy."

"I wouldn't say no," Defert smiled.

# CHAPTER 21

Bailiff Hershel Adrian called the case. "The United States versus Kerwood Wannamaker on the charge of murder."

Judge Parker addressed attorney Temple Houston. "Is the defense prepared?"

Temple stood in his white suit. "Thank you, Your Honor, for the time to gather witnesses. The defense is ready."

"Prosecution?"

Rupert Dalby got to his feet and took a rigid stance as he said, "The prosecution is ready, Your Honor."

"Then, let's proceed. Opening statements?"

Dalby stepped over and addressed the jury.

"Gentlemen of the jury — this is a simple, straight forward case of murder. Kenwood Wannamaker knowingly took the life of his young wife. He shot her in the back. The defendant has admitted his crime. We will prove that this man," Dalby pointed to the successful rancher dress in a white shirt and black suit sitting at the defense table, "deliberately slew a beautiful, vibrant young woman as she slept — in the very prime of her life. He knew what he was doing, and he intended to end the life of a righteous and honorable lady who had already suffered more than most of us will ever know. Her name was Leta "Golden

Flower." She had been captured by the Arapahoe when she was but twelve-years-old. The Army freed her at 18 — but only after she had been a slave and forced to marry an Arapahoe warrior. The man raped her repeatedly until she bore him a child."

Dalby turned and walked over toward Wannamaker and pointed a finger at him.

"Kerwood Wannamaker knew all of this, and yet he married her. He married her so he could murder her one day. Well, he did, and he should pay the ultimate price for it."

Dalby sat down, and Temple Houston got up.

"There is much more to this story than the prosecution has told you. We will reveal the multifaceted facts of this case, and you will see clearly that what Kerwood Wannamaker did was not only forgivable but justifiable. Please, gentlemen, open your minds to hear and understand the story we will lay before you. Thank you."

Houston took his seat, and Dalby quickly got back up.

"The prosecution offers in evidence this document," Dalby held up a single handwritten page of paper, "a full confession by the defendant. If it pleases the Court, we would like this tagged as prosecution Exhibit A."

"And this," Dalby held up a '73 Army single-action pistol and shoulder holster. "The prosecution would like to enter this into evidence as the murder weapon. This is Mr. Wannamaker's personal pistol, which he carried in this shoulder holster. Please may we have this marked Prosecution Exhibits B and C."

"Accepted," Judge Parker said, looking at the gun before handing it to Mr. Cross to be labeled.

"So ordered," Judge Parker said.

Then, as Dalby laid the page on the desk beside Court Clerk Presley Cross, he said, "The prosecution calls Dr. Alvah Haygood."

A middle-aged man with curly white hair rose and moved to the witness chair. Court Clerk, Presley Cross, swore in the short and thin physician. The doctor wore a suit with many, many miles on it. His dark eyes were bright and sharp.

"Dr. Haygood," prosecutor Dalby began, "can you provide the court with your credentials?"

"Of course," the doctor said, sitting up straight. "I have my medical degree from the School of Medicine at the University of Pennsylvania. I served as an Army surgeon during the war. I've been practicing in Van Buren for the last five years."

"And you were called to the Circle W ranch on the last day of July for what reason?"

"To examine the body of a young woman who had been shot and killed."

"The young woman was Leta Wannamaker?"

"Yes."

"Where was she shot?"

"In the back — between her shoulder blades, at thoracic vertebrae number 2. I believe that she died instantly."

"I show you this .44 caliber slug you recovered from the bedroom. Is this the bullet you found and do you believe it is the one which killed Mrs. Wannamaker. "

"Yes, it is," the doctor said, looking at the slug as it fell into his hand from a small manilla envelope. "This is my handwriting on the envelope."

"Thank you, Doctor," Dalby said, handing the envelope to the Court Clerk. "Please mark this Prosecution Exhibit D." Dalby returned to the prosecution table. "Your witness," he said to Houston.

Temple Houston looked down at his notes before he stepped over to the witness.

"Dr. Haygood, who summoned you to the Circle W?"

"The ranch foreman. I don't believe I know his name."

"For the record, Your Honor, the cowboy was Les Einhorn. And he is the foreman at the Circle W." Temple faced the jury as he asked, "From your observations, would you say that Mrs. Wannamaker was shot in her sleep?"

"That would be difficult to square with the facts."

"What facts? Wasn't the lady face down on the bed when you found her?"

"She was — but her face was in the pillow. If she were sleeping like that, she could not have been able to breathe."

"Any other facts you can tell us, Doctor?"

"The bullet which killed Mrs. Wannamaker passed through her body. There were no holes in the bed beneath her, where I would have expected to find one. Had she been shot laying in bed, the bullet would have left a mark on the mattress -- if not penetrate it completely."

"But you did find the bullet?"

"Yes. I dug it out of the wall between slats of the bed's headboard."

"So," Temple said, returning to the witness, "given where you found this bullet, what would you suspect was the position of the victim when shot?"

"My best guess is she was sitting up in bed — on her knees."

"And what was the state of dress of Mrs. Wannamaker when you found her?"

"Objection, Your Honor," Dalby shot to his feet. "This is intended to make a spectacle of the lady who is not here to defend herself."

"Your Honor," Temple said quickly, "the facts of the event will not change. All we are trying to do is establish those facts."

"I will allow it," Judge Parker said.

"The lady was naked," Dr. Haygood said.

"Did the body appear to have been moved in any way?"

"That I could not tell."

"Anything else unusual about the scene, Doctor?"

"Only that there was a dagger stuck in the mattress beside the victim's pillow."

"Was the blade stuck in deeply?"

"No. I'd say it looked as if it had been dropped and pierced the mattress only as much as the weapon's own weight would have brought."

Temple asked, "You are familiar with the layout of the Wanna-maker ranch house, are you not, Dr. Haywood? From your visits there over the years?"

"I think I am."

"Would you say that the victim was killed in the master bedroom?"

"No, sir. I found her across the hall and down in the last bedroom on the right."

"Thank you, Doctor Haywood. No more questions."

Rupert Dalby stood up, saying, "Redirect, Your Honor."

Judge Parker nodded his head.

"Dr. Haywood, do you believe the knife you found would have been any defense against a .44 caliber pistol?"

"No, sir, I wouldn't."

"Any rebuttal, Mr. Houston," Judge Parker asked.

"No, your honor." To Dr. Haywood, Houston said, "Thank you."

"The witness is dismissed," Judge Parker said. After another moment, the Judge said, "This trial is adjourned until tomorrow morning."

# CHAPTER 22

The first thing the next day, the Prosecution rested its murder case against rancher Kerwood Wannamaker. Dr. Haygood had been its only witness. The written confession of Wanna-maker and the bullet that killed his wife, the only physical evidence submitted.

"Your Honor," Temple Houston said, ready to present the full case for the defense, "the defense calls Mr. Elmo Rigsdill to the stand."

A tradesman, Rigsdill was five foot six inches and a little heavy for a man of his height. But his weight was muscle instead of fat. He wore bib overalls and a pink shirt that used to be red. A thatch of wiry brown whiskers covered his face.

Rigsdill was sworn in by Presley Cross and took the witness chair with his straw hat in his hands.

"Mr. Rigsdill," Temple Morgan said, crossing to the witness chair, "what is your profession?"

"Saddlemaker."

"And the name of your business?"

"Rigsdill Brothers Saddlery."

"Where is your brother?"

There was a pause while the witness took a deep breath. When he spoke again, he said, "Orley's dead. I killed him when he shot me." Unbid, the man slipped the left strap off his shoulder and unbuttoned two buttons of his shirt. He pulled the cloth aside to show an ugly scar over his collarbone. "This is where he hit me."

"Where did this shooting happen?"

"Over by The Dove House."

"Let the record show," Temple said as Elmo rebuttoned his shirt and pulled the strap of his overalls back in place, "The Dove House is a house of ill-repute."

"And the reason for the fight between you and your brother," Temple asked, turning back to the witness?

"Golden Flower, she called herself."

"A soiled dove?"

"A dirty scheming female witch!"

"Your Honor," Prosecutor Dalby said, leaning forward with his fingers spread on the prosecution table, "I object to his testimony. This is an attempt to besmirch the character of a lady who is not able to defend honor."

"Her profession speaks for her *honor*," Temple said. "And, Your Honor, as to the character of Mrs. Wannamaker, the Prosecution opened that door for questioning. In his opening remarks, Mr. Dalby referring to her as '...*a righteous and honorable lady*.' It is our purpose to prove that the woman Kerwood Wannamaker married and killed was neither."

"Objection sustained," Judge Parker said and rapped his gavel to signal he would book no further comment on the matter. "The defense may continue."

"Mr. Rigssdill," Temple asked the witness, "am I to presume that you and your brother *knew* Mrs. Wannamaker — *intimately* at The Dove House?"

"I am ashamed to say we did. Both me and Orley were regular customers of that sinful place. And she wasn't Mrs. Wannamaker when we knew her. She jest called herself Golden Flower."

"How did the scrap between you and your brother occur?"

"She spun us both up. She told us she loved us and wanted each of us to take her away from the terrible life she was in. She told us to meet her at the same time one night out the back of The Dove House. She also told both of us to bring a gun to make sure she could get away. When Orley and I met, we asked each other what he was doin' there. Turned out, we was there fer th' same reason. We argued, and he pulled his gun and shot me. I was bleeding on the ground when I killed my brother."

Elmo Rigsdill took a few moments to compose himself. With no more prompting from Temple, Elmo continued. "She never came to see me when I was laid up — she didn't go to Orley's funeral. I got word from the Professor at The Dove House that she never wanted to see me again."

"Are you sure there was no mistake between you and your brother — or between either of you and — Golden Flower?"

"No mistake. She wanted us to meet — armed — and to fight over her. I'm sure of it."

"Your witness," Temple Houston said to Rupert Dalby. The prosecutor had no questions.

When Rigsdill had left the courtroom, Temple called three other witnesses. A sister who had lost her brother in a fight with a gambler over Golden Flower, then Claxton Landers, and Joseph (Pick) Pickering the editors of Ft. Smith's two newspapers. From both of the reporters/editors, he got printed stories of other men who had died in knife fights and gunfights — over Golden Flower. Copies of those stories were entered into evidence.

Lastly, Temple called Miss Jewell Back. Without attempting to incriminate the owner, Temple was able to obtain confirmation of Golden Flower's manipulation of men before she left The Dove House.

"Do you have any opinion — and I assure the Court and the Jury that I am aware I am asking for speculation on Golden Flower — but I am doing so from a source who would have such knowledge if anyone would — why the woman in question did what she did?"

"Objection!" Dalby shouted.

"Objection noted, Mr. Prosecutor, but I will determine if this testimony is relevant after we hear it," Judge Parker said. To the witness, he said, "You may continue."

"Golden Flower was her Arapahoe name. When I pressed her, she said her white name was Leta Smith. I would have no way of knowing if that were true or not. As I'm sure you do know, she was kidnapped as a child and worked as a slave before she was forced to marry an Arapahoe brave. She told me she was raped repeatedly by her Indian husband before and even during her pregnancy. She bore a son. It was soon afterward that the Army rescued her. She left the child and told me she never cared for him in the least. She kept her Indian name because she was not accepted back into white society after her years, marriage and having a child by an Indian. She told me prostitution was the only work she was able to get. She knew she was pretty — but she had a deep hatred for all white men. It is my opinion that she wanted men to fight to the death over her. She was glad the Rigsdill brothers tied to do that for her — however, she never cared for one of them."

The Judge considered Miss Bach's remarks a few moments before announcing, the testimony is allowed to stand.

"Thank you, Your Honor," Temple said.

Back to his witness, he said, "Are you aware of how Mr. Wannamaker and Leta came to be married?"

"I know that after I refused to have her around anymore, she somehow met Kerwood Wannamaker within a matter of days."

"He was a regular customer?"

"Not regular. He had loved his first wife, Blanche. When she died of the wasting disease, he was a man without a purpose, I think. When he met, Golden Flower — or Leta as she was calling herself then — he was struck like many men are. I'm sure it didn't take much for her to get him to marry her and take her away from everything."

"Thank you, Miss Bach," Temple said. "Mr. Dalby?"

Dalby tried to get Jewel Bach to admit that she ran two houses of prostitution, but she claimed her Fifth Amendment right against self-incrimination. Finally, the Prosecution gave up. The Judge dismissed the witness

"Your Honor," Temple said, "We have only one more witness to call — but as this has been a long day, may I suggest a recess until tomorrow. This testimony will be difficult to hear."

"It has been a trying day, Mr. Houston," Judge Parker said, rapping his gavel on this desk. "Court is adjourned until after lunch."

# CHAPTER 23

"Regretfully, Your Honor, the defense calls Tyler Wannamaker to the stand."

It was the afternoon Temple Houston had promised to call his last witness in the murder trial.

From the back of the courtroom, a young man stood, his head hung. The boy walked to the witness chair in the slightly awkward gait of a teenager. He dressed in slacks and a pressed shirt. He took the oath from Presley Cross, the Court Clerk, before he sat in the witness chair.

"May it please the court," white-suited defense attorney Houston said to Judge Parker. "This testimony will be embarrassing for the witness but also for Your Honor and the jury to hear. With that in mind, I request some latitude from the court. I want to be able to ask some leading questions of the witness — leading so that I may seek the needed information without overloading this young man. I also request the indulgence of Mr. Dalby because the story that must be told here is mortifying. I will attempt to cover everything, but if I miss something, the Prosecution may address it in his cross-examination."

Judge Parker narrowed his eyes a moment before saying, "I will allow you as much scope as possible. And I will ask the Prosecution to be as tolerant as possible. Proceed, Mr. Houston."

"Thank you, Your Honor."

To the witness, Temple said, "Mr. Tyler Wannamaker, your age is fourteen, is it not?"

"Yes," the young man said almost in a whisper.

"The witness will need to speak up," the Judge admonished the teen.

"Yes, sir," the boy said louder.

"You are the only living child of Blanche and the defendant, Kerwood Wannamaker."

"Yes, sir," he said.

"You had a sister who died at birth and an older brother who was thrown from a horse. He died as a result of the accident, didn't he?"

"Yes, sir."

"You were very close to your mother, were you not?"

"Yes, sir."

"She died what — six — almost seven years ago of consumption? Correct?"

"Yes, sir."

"Your father took the death of your brother and sister as well as your mother very hard, did he not?"

"Yes, sir."

"Would you characterize your father in recent years as — alive but not really living?"

The boy nodded his head and bit his lip before the said, "Yes, sir."

"The first time you met your new stepmother was the day your father returned to the ranch with her, wasn't it?"

"Yes."

"And the very next day, didn't your father take his new wife on a honeymoon to New York City?"

"Yes."

"They did not return for a month, correct?"

"Yes."

"Now, this is the difficult part, Tyler, but I need your answers loud and clear."

The teen clenched his jaw and took a breath as he lifted his head.

Temple Houston took a moment before he asked his next question.

"You avoided your stepmother — even moving your room to one at the very end of the hall, didn't you?"

"Yes, sir."

"Did your stepmother do things to make you uncomfortable?"

"Yes."

"Did she flirt with you — embarrass you coming out of the bathroom or even the master bedroom less than fully dressed?"

The boy had to take a breath before he nodded his head as he said, "Yes."

"Did she try to flirt with you even when your father was around?"

"Yes."

"Was there a time when she removed her shoe — and under the dining table used her foot to stroke the inside of your leg above your knee?"

Tyler Wannamaker flushed red and even shivered before he looked down as he answered. "Yes."

"Did you try to stay away from the ranch house and, in particular, your stepmother?"

"Yes, sir," the boy said, still looking down.

"Did you ever speak about what was going on to your father — or to anyone?"

"No, sir," Tyler said, slumping his shoulders.

"So, to the best of your knowledge, your father was unaware of what was happening between you and your stepmother."

"Yes, sir."

"The day of — let's call it the '*incident*' — your father had left the ranch early to consult with his banker in Van Buren, did he not?"

"Yes, sir."

"You were awakened in your bed by your stepmother, correct?"

"Yes," the boy said slowly.

"Your stepmother was naked, was she not?"

The boy had to close his eyes to answer the question. "Yes, sir."

"Did your stepmother climb into your bed — naked — and seduce you?"

Tears came to Tyler's eyes as he again blushed red. He had to choke back a sob as he said, "Yes, sir."

Temple turned to the jury and said, "A young teenage boy — a woman who had worked as a soiled dove for several years — naked — seduced this teen — who among us could have resisted?"

It was a rhetorical question, and after it hung in the court unanswered, Temple turned back to young Tyler.

"The way of nature is that — after being spent — one sleeps. Did you go to sleep while your stepmother was in your bed?"

The boy had to swallow before he could say, "Yes."

"Now, Tyler, I need you to answer the next questions with more than a single word." Temple paused before he began once more. "What was the next thing you remember."

"I — I woke up — when my father fired his pistol."

"What did you see when you awoke?"

"My stepmother — her mouth open — in shock — a bloody hole in her chest —." There appeared to be more the boy had to say.

Temple encouraged him, "And what else, Tyler? Tell us?"

It took a few moments before the teen could force himself to say, "She had a knife in her hand."

"A knife. A butcher knife — a Bowie knife — a dagger?"

"A dagger."

"She then fell towards you, obviously — what did you do?"

"I rolled out of her way. She fell into the pillow."

"And the knife?"

"She dropped it, and it stuck into the mattress."

Temple paced to the jury and back to the prosecution table. Then he looked up at Judge Parker.

"Thank you, Your Honor, for your patience and leeway. Mr. Dalby, your witness."

Rupert Dalby studied the boy as Temple sat down. Then to the Judge, the prosecutor said, "No questions, Your Honor."

# CHAPTER 24

Both Ft. Smith newspapers went to press carrying news of the closing arguments in the Wannamaker trial.

The Vindicator detailed Rupert Dalby's remarks.

"This is still, as I told you in the beginning, a straightforward case. Kerwood Wannamaker murdered his new wife. He shot her in the back and killed her. You've seen the gun, the very bullet, and the signed confession of the defendant.

"As a jury, your task is clear and simple as well. Find this man guilty of the crime to which he has admitted — murder."

The Ft. Smith Ledger focused more on Temple Houston's closing statement.

"Put yourself in the boots of Kerwood Wannamaker. He is a man who lost his first wife and suffered the grief of that loss for years. Then totally unexpected he met a striking and alluring young woman, Leta Smith — no one knows her real last name — but many men know her as Golden Flower. She was white but claimed to be Indian. Why? I believe it's because of her kidnapping and mistreatment at the hands of the Arapahoe. She did this because even after the Army rescued her — after years of abuse — she was considered '*damaged goods*' by her family and community. Because of this, she turned to the oldest profession in the world with a burning hatred of the white race. She considered herself still an Indian and chose to wreak savage revenge on every white man she could. You've heard the testimony from two respected newspaper editors recounting other occasions in which men lost their lives through the manipulations of — Golden Flower.

"Kerwood took his feelings for this woman to be love, and when she responded, he fell in love with her and quickly married her, knowing that she had been a soiled dove. He took her on a grand honeymoon to New York City and made her the mistress of his successful ranch when they returned.

"But unknown to him, the vengeful woman, this black widow spider, was spinning her web to destroy the one man who had accepted her without conditions. She played her seduction on Kerwood's teenage son — a boy not worldly-wise nor sophisticated. His new stepmother flirted with him, even exposed herself to him — all to stir his lust.

"Tyler Wannamaker was made of sterner stuff, and as best he could, he ignored her — even moving his room as far away from his father and his new stepmother's bedroom as he could. Then early one day, when his father had gone to town, the boy awoke to a naked and voluptuous woman climbing into his bed. Satan's powers are strong — and the young man was overwhelmed and succumbed to his stepmother.

"When she finally exhausted him, and he fell asleep, she straddled him, produced a dagger, and was prepared to plunge the blade into the boy's heart — something that, together with her seduction of his son, would surely wrecked and drown Kerwood in shame and guilt.

"However, Kerwood returned to his ranch and to the scene of his planned ruin — only moments before Golden Flower could complete her despicable acts. He stopped her before she could kill his only living child — and he did it the only way he could in that instant. He pulled his pistol and shot her as she was poised above his son with a dagger in her hand.

"Put yourself in Kerwood Wannamaker's boots. What would you have done?"

There was little doubt in any reader's mind, regardless of which paper they might have read, what had occurred on the Circle W. The headlines of both newspapers proclaimed that the case was now in the hands of the jury.

\* \* \*

When Judge Parker returned to the bench almost two days later, the jury for the Wannamaker case was there waiting for him. The Judge gaveled the court of order and asked, "Mr. Foreman, has the jury reached its verdict?"

A man in a suit straining at its buttons stood in the jury box.

"No, Your Honor. After a day and a half of deliberation — we are unable to reach a unanimous verdict."

Kerwood Wannamaker clutched his attorney's arm, wondering what this meant. Temple Houston spoke a few words in his client's ear. His words didn't seem to calm the defendant.

After giving the matter some thought, the Judge asked the jury, ""Do you think, another day of deliberation would enable you to reach consensus?"

"I'm sorry, Your Honor. I don't believe so. The division is hard drawn."

Judge Parker sighed before he said, "Well, I want to thank you, gentlemen, of the jury for your efforts. The jury is dismissed."

Rupert Dalby stood up as he spoke, "Your Honor, the prosecution moves for a mistrial and requests a new trial date."

Wannamaker grabbed Temple's shoulder, shaking his head.

When the defense attorney rose, he said, "Your Honor, this has been a devastating time for the defendant and his son — as I'm sure the court understands."

"Not as devastating as it was on the victim," Dalby shot back.

"May it please the court," Temple said after a quick few words with Wannamaker, "the defense moves for a directed verdict from the bench."

The jury walked out, and the courtroom was silent for a few moments before Judge Parker spoke.

"The court will deliberate overnight and issue a directed verdict tomorrow morning."

* * *

First-time Deputy Raul Vega returned to Ft. Smith from Durant in the Choctaw part of the Indian Territory with John Browneagle. The two led four horses with War Dog, and the other three arrested remains of his renegade gang. They rode up to the jail below the courthouse.

Peg legged Deputy Stonewall Welch and jailer Herb Irwin awaited the riders. The overweight and hulking, Irwin unlocked the barred jail door keeping his shotgun in the crook of his arm.

Stonewall pulled his revolver and helped untie and dismount the prisoners while Raul Vega and John Browneagle guided the Indians into the lockup.

The last and the youngest of the prisoners was Bear Killer. He tried to kick Stonewall as he dismounted, but the Deputy was too quick. The lawman dodged the kick, cocked his pistol as he stuck it in the rash brave's ribs.

Beady eyes and pale-skinned Herb Irwin unlocked the handcuffs on each prisoner as he passed through the steel barred door. But the moment one hand was free, Bear Killer shoved Irwin back and used the door to batter Vega and Browneagle. He threw a hard elbow into Stonewall's face before leaping over the one-legged man and racing across the open parade ground in front of the courthouse and jail.

Stonewall managed to snatch Vega's Henry rifle and chamber a round as the young buck sprinted away. The hangman/Deputy Marshal put a slug between the fleeing Indian's shoulder blades. The young man spread his arms out wide, arched his chest forward, and fell to the grass dead.

Irwin locked the jail door as both Vega and Browneagle hurried after the escape. Stonewall ran after them, levering another round into the rifle.

Bear Killer was dead before he hit the grass.

Standing over the body, Vega said, "Well, at least he won't hang."

"But," Stonewall said, "runnin' away like this ain't what I'd call a warrior's death."

# CHAPTER 25

Bailiff Hershel Adrian loudly said, "The defendant will stand and face the court.

Kerwood Wannamaker got to his feet, and Temple Houston stood beside him.

The Judge looked through his notes for a moment and then said, "It is apparent that the defendant did shoot and kill his wife." A few more moments passed before the Judge went on. "The facts of this case are — nothing like we have ever encountered. The killing of one human being by another is the most serious accusation this bench ever faces. Given the fact, that there was a confession by the defendant with the shocking story behind it — this court finds Mr. Kerwood Wannamaker not guilty by reason of justified homicide."

The Judge wrapped his gavel, and it was over.

"Call the next case," Judge Parker said.

The Court Clerk stood and said, "The United States of America vs. Clemente Bays, on the charges of making and selling alcohol in the Indian Territory — and bigamy."

A new jury shuffled in.

Kerwood collapsed into his seat, his head in his hands sobbing. Temple sat down and put a hand on his client's back.

When he could, Wannamaker looked up through tear-filled eyes and said, "I thought for sure they'd hang me." He took a couple of breaths. "What in the world do I do now?"

\* \* \*

Out on the courthouse porch, Kerwood Wannamaker shared an awkward hug with his son Tyler.

"Pa," the boy said with tears in his eyes, "I am so sorry. Can you ever forgive me?"

"Tyler, you are my son," Kerwood said. "You were a victim. Leta used me, and she used you against me. You are young, and this should never have happened to you."

"What can I do?" the boy asked.

"Go home, son. You still have a lot of growing up to do. And you have a ranch to learn how to run.

"Les," Kerwood said to his foreman, Les Einhorn, "I want you to move into the house. This is your home, too. And I want you to know when you retire there will always be a rocking chair waiting for you. But for now, I want you to go back to doing your job and take Tyler under your wing. Teach him what he needs to know. Let him do every job on the spread."

"You're not coming back?" the foreman asked.

"From time to time. But not right now. This had been such a damaging thing that's happened to us all. I think it would be easier if I let you run the ranch and teach Tyler how to do it himself one day. I'm not coming back to the ranch right now. I'll be back — from time to time — but not right now."

"Then that's the way it'll be," Einhorn said, shaking Kerwood's hand. "Tyler, let's get back to work," he said to the boy.

"Yes, sir," Tyler said. He hesitated for a second and then turned and followed the foreman.

Temple Houston stepped up to his client and said, "How about a drink?"

"I think I'm ready. And I'd like your advice about what I should do legally to ensure that the ranch goes to Tyler — no matter what I do or where I go."

"I can do that. Do you have any ideas about what you want to do next?"

* * *

"A proposal?" Delta asked as she smiled.

"That was what he said. 'I'd like to ask you to have supper with me this evening at The Craig House to discuss a proposal.'" Mena was getting dressed for the occasion.

"What do you think about it?" Delta wanted to know.

"I think we'd be a good match. We enjoy each other's company — and we work well together."

"But has there been anything romantic between you?" Mena's best friend asked.

"He's almost kissed me twice."

"Almost?"

"One thing I've learned about Claxton is that he doesn't do anything until he's sure."

"And he isn't sure, yet?"

"I think he is. I suspect that's why he's being so bold."

Delta clapped her hands quietly in glee. "I've not said anything — but I've seen some of the looks he gives you, Mena. And the way you look at him."

"Well, it's not like it was with Benson. It's different — but the same — maybe even a little deeper."

"I understand," Delta said. "It's the way I feel about Mace."

"And I think he feels the same."

"So do I. But neither of us is in a rush."

"I haven't been with Claxton for very long, either."

"But tonight might be the night."

"Yes, I think it will be."

* * *

The Craig House was lovely as ever. Still the best place in Ft. Smith to eat. It had linen table cloths, silver flatware, and simple but elegant china plates, cups, and saucers. The whole place was bathed in the soft light of lanterns and candles. It was inviting and romantic.

Claxton Landers had picked Mena up at her front door and spoken to Delta, who was keeping Mena's two girls. He had a stick of candy for both Milly and Martha. They both hugged him and ran off to enjoy their treat.

"You two have fun," Delta said as they walked off.

Now, seated in a corner where they had some privacy, they ordered dinner and enjoyed a glass of wine.

"I hired a new reporter," Claxton said nervously. "Young man who wants to write — maybe novels, maybe short stories — but he knows he needs some experience."

"What's his name?" Mena asked.

"Auston Laughinghouse."

"Laughinghouse?" Mena couldn't help but giggle.

"I've already told him he'll have to come up with a shorter pseudonym. Auston Laughinghouse takes too much space and too long to put into type."

"Has he done it yet?"

"That's his first assignment. That and meeting all the incoming paddlewheels and stagecoaches tomorrow."

They enjoyed a wonderful dinner. They laughed and talked seriously about the Wannamaker trial.

When they finished their meal, they relaxed with another glass of wine.

After some silence, Claxton finally said, "You know how well we've been doing with the paper. I mean, you keep the books?"

"Yes," she said, not pressing him.

"Well — what would you think about —," he took a deep breath, " — going from twice a week to three times a week? Tuesday, Thursday, and Saturday?"

This was not what Mena expected at all. She blinked twice without speaking.

"We have the ads to cover it — and if we keep three pages for each issue — we can double our income within a year," he said.

Mena sat back, holding her wine glass.

"What do you think? Could you keep up with the recipes and the Aunt Hildegarde columns? I could give the new guy the obits."

There was silence between the pair for a few moments.

"I can't do this without you, Mena. Of course, there's a raise for you — I'll even double your salary."

Mena put her glass down and wiped her mouth.

"What do you want, Mena?" Claxton said, sitting forward.

Mena gave the idea a thought before she said, "What I want, Claxton, is half ownership in the paper."

"What?" he said in shock. "Half?"

"You know I can do everything you do — set type, work the press — and write."

Claxton could not find the words to respond.

Finally, Mena said slowly, "Or — ."

"Or what?"

"Or — a marriage license and a ring."

Claxton sank back into his chair. It took a full minute before he sat forward again and said, "How about — how about all three?"

# CHAPTER 26

.

Four Deputy Marshals marched the five men to be executed out of jail, across the parade ground, and past the gathered crowd to the gallows. Each man had his hands shackled behind his back. They were ushered up the thirteen steps to the platform above. There each was directed to stand by under a noose already waiting for him. The gallows itself was painted white and had a steeply raked roof.

Once in place, Stonewall stepped up behind each man, and buckled a belt around the prisoner's knees and placed the hemp rope over his head, resting the carefully braided knot on the man's left shoulder.

While this was being done, Bailiff Hershel Adrian read the Death Warrant for each of the convicted. He also asked each man if he had any last words. None of them did.

The last part of the ceremony was to place a black sack over each man's head.

"I don't need any damn sack," poisoner Esau Falzon snarled.

"It ain't fer you," Stonewall said. "We don't want folks to have to look at you when you piss your pants and shit yourself." The hangman yanked the bag down over Falzon's face.

Mace stood at one end of the gallows, his arms crossed as Stonewall finished his duties. Lastly, the one-legged Deputy Marshal walked to the far end of the gallows and put both his hands on a wooden lever. He looked over at Mace. Mace nodded his head, and the hangman wrenched the lever backward. The floor below the condemned men split open, and they all fell. The pop of their broken necks was not heard beyond the immediate vicinity of the gallows, but all the men jerked and swung slightly. There was no kicking or squirming. They all died in an instant.

The crowd gasped, and some turned away as the prisoners dropped.

The Deputies who had guarded the doomed men on their last walk, now worked together to release them from their ropes. The lawmen lay the bodies out into waiting simple board caskets. These boxes were then loaded into the bed wagons parked nearby.

The crowd drifted away.

* * *

The restaurant where Mace ate with Delta was just called Steaks. It had once been a rougher and raucous place for mostly men and working girls. However, it had evolved into a more family welcoming place. This is due to the excellent cooking and steadily growing success of the place.

Delta drank iced tea, and Mace had coffee. As they ate, they talked.

"I couldn't believe it," Delta said with a smile. "What woman asks a man to marry her?"

"My sister," Mace said with a chuckle. "She probably saved them six months to a year's worth of time by being direct."

"I'll agree with you on that. Do you think they'll be a good match?"

"I have no doubt."

"Me either. I think most folks who came into the paper thought so too — for months before either Mena or Claxton did."

They ate for a few moments.

"You're not going to have to ask me," Mace said when he finished eating.

"Oh?" Delta smiled.

"How about when I get back from this next trip?"

"Are we talking about a June wedding? I wouldn't want to take anything away from Mena and Claxton's big day."

"Have they set a date?"

"Valentine's Day."

"That should be easy for him to remember."

Delta finished her meal. The waitress took their plates and asked if either wanted cake for dessert. Neither did. But they did want more to drink. The waitress left and returned to fill both their tea and coffee.

"Do I know your new partner?" Delta asked.

"I don't think you've met him — but you know of him. Kerwood Wannamaker."

"No, we've not met."

"You'll like him. Of course, these days, he's not very sociable."

"Understandable."

"He was a sheriff down in Texas before the war," Mace said, leaning forward. "He tells me he goes on the trail with each herd he sends to market. He knows how hard the ground is and how to keep a cold camp when it's required."

"When did you decide to go out with him?"

"There are more warrants on my desk than all the Deputies can deal with already. I've been thinking about taking some of the load myself. Then when Temple Houston asked me to meet him at The Sidewheeler, Wannamaker was there. He said he was looking for something to do — something away from his ranch — and something worth his doing. He seemed like a good fit. So I invited him to go with me. While we're out, we're going to be on the lookout for other possible Deputies. It will be good to have someone else's opinion."

* * *

Kerwood Wannamaker waited for Mace to show up at Wendorff's Livery at first light. The new deputy's dark bay was saddled and ready. The livery owner, Rollo Wendorff, had a blue roan for the Marshal and a mouse dun as a packhorse. The later was fitted with a double crosstree packsaddle. The animal's attachment was loaded with the gear and supplies Mace had specified.

"No tumbleweed wagon?" Rollo asked, referring to the rolling jail cell most Deputy Marshals took with them.

"They're all in use," Mace said. "The last few deputies I sent out had to go without them, too. I've ordered some more made but none are ready yet. If we have to, we'll get one built for us along the way — and hire a driver and cook."

Kerwood said, "Guess we do with what we've got."

"That we do."

"Where to first?"

Mace pulled out five warrants from his inside coat pocket. There was a slight chill in the air, and both men were dressed for any unexpected change in the weather.

"Cherokee country," Mace said, meaning the northeast corner of the Indian Territory. "Tahlequah, to be exact."

"I've been there. Not a bad town."

"Nope," Mace said, swinging into his saddle, "but then we go to Tulsey Town."

Kerwood then took the reins of the packhorse from Rollo.

"Good huntin', gents," Rollo said.

"Tulsey Town," Kerwood said. "Now, that's a bad place."

"Which is why we're going there," Mace said, as the two rode off.

## THE END

BONUS

Six Chapter from

**INCIDENT AT LAJITAS**

# CHAPTER ONE

Clay Maxwell paid his bill at the registration desk of the Menger Hotel. This was the best San Antonio had to offer. Built in 1859 William Menger built the structure next to his brewery which happened to be next to the remains of the Alamo.

It had been only the day before the 6 foot 3 inch lawman had turned his Texas Ranger star in at the Austin Ranger's headquarters after 20 years of service. He had made the 80 mile trek from the Texas capital to the site of the Alamo that same day.

Rested and ready to begin the rest of his life the next morning, he wore a faded gray but clean shirt, and his weathered leather jacket. He paid the 4 dollar charge to the clerk behind the waist high highly polished mahogany counter.

"It's been a pleasure to have you with us, Captain Maxwell," the clerk said. "Your horse is saddled and waiting for you out front."

The clean shaven former Ranger didn't bother to correct the title. He knew he'd always be known to some as Captain Maxwell. But to himself, he was now simply Clay Maxwell.

"Thank you," he said picking up a match from the holder on the counter, he turned toward the street.

"Captain Clay Maxwell!" a boisterous man in a black suit and flat crowned hat said from across the lobby. "Pride of the Texas Rangers," he added as he climbed out of a padded chair. He pulled back his coat to allow him access to the revolver he wore in a holster strapped to his leg. The man had a thin dark mustache above the sneer he wore revealing yellowed teeth.

"No longer a ranger," Maxwell said. "Just retired."

"Don't matter to us," another man said stepping out from behind one of a dozen pillars in the lobby. He stepped into the center of the tiled floor below the stained glass ceiling two floors above. This man was not as dapper has his partner. He wore jeans and a plaid shirt. He carried his pistol on his left hip.

"'The man that killed Clay Maxwell' is all people are going to remember," said the fancy man.

"Which one of you is that going to be?" Maxwell said while chewing on his match.

"Both of us," the dusty, sandy haired one said. He hadn't shaved in a good week.

"At least one of you is going to die," Maxwell said. The clerk eased out from behind his counter and Maxwell. "Most likely both of you."

Both of the men laughed a very unfunny laugh.

"Oh, we heard you were fast – but no one is fast enough to get us both," the more dirty of the two said.

"Let's say you get, lucky, and you do kill me. Which ain't likely," Maxwell said. "But say you do. Then which one of you is going to be the one to back shoot the other?"

The pair didn't grasp what the big man was saying?

"There can only be one – 'man who killed Clay Maxwell' – even if it takes two of you to get it done. So – sooner or later, one of you is going to shoot the other – most likely in the dark, in the back."

The two gunmen exchanged looks calculating what his changes were. But quickly they turned back to their prey.

By this time Maxwell had his right hand down and used his thumb to push the thong off the hammer of his Colt. He was ready.

"You can't get us both," the mustached man said.

"That's your plan?"

"That's a cold hard fact," the other man said.

"Well, it's for sure I'm going to kill whoever moves first. What you have to figure out is, how do you wait just long enough so I'm busy with your partner and you can get your shot off."

The eyes of both men darted back and forth. Maxwell had gotten into their minds.

"No," the man in the suit finally said, "whoever moves first gets the first shot off."

"But he won't live to see how well he did. Maybe he was so quick he actually ended up shooting into the floor. But before he can get off another shot, I've already killed him."

"Let's just see," the left handed gunman said.

It was his partner in the suit who moved first.

What neither believed was just how fast Clay Maxwell was. He put a slug into the center chest of the white shirt and dropped to his knee and fanned his second shot into the other gunman who did get a shot off. Unfortunately that slug buried itself into the hotel's check in counter.

Both men lost the grip on their pistols as their vision shifted up to the stain glass ceiling and they hit the floor.

Maxwell got back to his feet and checked both bodies before he holstered his weapon. Was this what was retirement was going to be like?

One thing was for damn sure. They were never going to let him back in the Menger again.

# CHAPTER TWO

Three riders were silhouetted against the first glow of an approaching summer desert morning. Two were Mexicans in wide sombreros. The third was a Comanche — more like a Comanchero — the trash that was full blooded Indian but lived like a scavenger. The three men moved purposefully until they pulled up at the bank of the slowly flowing Rio Grande. They allowed their horses a drink.

One of the riders, Rafael, also wore a vest and grimy shirt without buttons. He was the leader of this advance party. He sat in his large pummel Mexican saddle and rolled himself a smoke. He struck a match to it and took a couple of drags. Next to him Valente took a drink from his canteen. The second bandit had a dirty but ruffled shirt and a fully loaded bandolero over one shoulder and across his chest.

The prematurely grey, Iron Hair, sat silently while his horse drank. He wore no head gear except a red scarf tied around his head. He, too, had on a vest, but wore a breach cloth instead of pants under his gun belt. He had moccasins that reached up to his mid-calf.

After a couple of drags Rafael flipped the cigarette butt into the water. The three men checked their pistols, then returned the weapons to their holsters, and moved out across the river.

The riders stepped into the water up to their stirrups and emerged on the hard-rock bank and slipped back into the darkness of the rugged country. Their horses quietly stepped through the gloom as little more than shadows.

\* \* \*

Out from the boulders and rough hewn desert stood an elegant hacienda. There was also a bunkhouse and barn, along with a storage building. Some distance from the house was a corral.

In the corral was a single horse — a magnificent animal which nervously pranced around the enclosure.

On foot, Rafael stepped through the gate and approached the horse with a lasso in hand. Valente, still in the saddle, held the gate while managing Rafael's mount. Iron Hair kept watch.

Rafael threw the rope and snared the stallion. The man made a halter of the rope and slipped it over the animal's head. He led the stallion out handing the lasso to Valente. Rafael vaulted into his saddle and took back the rope. Quietly the three carefully whisked their prize away. They quickly disappeared into the distance, their dust settling as the sun made its first appearance over the mountains.

A rooster crowed on one of the fence posts, and the day was ready to begin on the ranch.

# CHAPTER THREE

The door to the barn opened and out stepped Pepi, a Mexican boy of seven. He wore a loose simple over-the-head cotton shirt and matching pants. Barefooted he yawned as he struggled with two buckets of feed he had filled from a bin in the barn.

He walked toward the corral and absent-mindedly pushed the gate closed. Glancing toward the corral his eyes popped as he searched the space. Pepi almost dropped the buckets of feed to the ground as he peered through the rail fence and then looked in all directions.

The corral was empty.

The realization hit the boy that the prize horse was actually gone. His mouth dropped open, and he ran off to the adobe bunkhouse.

"Señor Tom!! Señor Tom!!" he yelled as he raced into the long building.

It was semi-dark inside as burlap curtains covered the windows. The room was crowded with bunks, which sagged under the weight of numb ranch hands. They were snoring and trying to sleep off the effects of the previous night. There was evidence of some sort of celebration still strewn across the floor — empty whiskey bottles, cards, boots and clothes.

Pepi slid to a stop in front of a door to the private room at the back of the bunkhouse. The boy threw it open and found Tom Kelso. The ranch foreman was in his early 50's, an old cowboy whose skin was leathered by the years. His body only now beginning to show its years.

"Señor Tom!! Señor Tom!!" the boy hollered again.

Kelso tried to sit up at the sound of his name. He pushed his Montana peak styled hat from over his face — his hang-over exploded in his head and he froze. He recovered a moment later and got to his feet in his long handles.

Pepi had already turned and started racing back up the path between the bunks when Kelso struggled to his door. As quickly as his throbbing head would allow, he followed the boy.

When Tom Kelso made it to the open door of the bunkhouse, he stood squinting at the rays of the sun from the small porch. Pepi, yelled once more.

"Señor, Tom!! El Caballo!"

Kelso held his aching head and managed to say, "What?"

The boy said, "Se robaron el caballo!"

The foreman pried his eyes open as much as he could.

"Stolen?"

Then the magnitude of what the child was saying struck him.

"Trafalgar?"

"Si!"

They both took off running, the older man sometimes hobbling on rocks, which didn't appear to bother the boy.

Pepi pulled up at the edge of the corral followed quickly by Kelso. The cowboy held his hand up to protect his eyes against the rising sun. Kelso pulled the gate open and dropped to one knee. He studied the tracks in the hard dirt.

The marks of four horses led off the ranch to the South. Kelso followed the marks with his eyes until he was looking off in the distance. Pepi stepped up behind Kelso.

The boy asked, "¿Se han ido hace mucho tiempo, Señor Tom?"

"Nope. Not long. Not from the looks of these."

Kelso stood and hurried back toward the bunkhouse.

# CHAPTER FOUR

Kelso rushed through the bunkhouse in his long johns, kicking bunks and poking sleeping cowboys as he went.

"Get up!! Off your ass!!

The cowboys grumble but Kelso yells, "Everybody up!!"

Buck Lyle, one of the ranch hands, late 30's, scruffy, bloodshot eyes, and about a month behind in shaving and bathing, jerked up in his bed. "What in th' hell!!" Then Buck grabbed his head by covering both ears and grimacing.

Kelso, called over his shoulder as he hot footed it across the wooden floor, "Lord Bristol's horse is gone!"

"My God!" Curly reacted looking for his shirt. The maybe 30, maybe 40, short, muscular, black cowboy with long tangled hair, slammed his eyes closed as he sat up on the side of his bed. He opened one eye and searched for his boots.

In his room, Kelso pulled on his pants, jerked on his boots and reached for his shirt on the floor. He grabbed his vest, which held a watch on a fob, and a double barreled shotgun from behind the door.

Clint Foster, 20, got to his feet still in his clothes and hat. He reached for his boots, shook them out, and pulled them on.

* * *

Only a few minutes later Kelso and his crew, Buck, Curly, young Clint, and three more cowboys pulled to a stop at the river bank. Kelso looked across the river.

Iron Hair sat in his saddle, a leg slung over his saddle horn. He held a rifle in the air, its butt against his thigh.

Kelso swallowed slowly and got a slight pain in his chest. However, he narrowed his eyes and pulled back the hammers of his shotgun. Then Kelso spurred his horse into the river. Only Buck and Clint quickly followed Kelso's lead. Curly and the others held back, thinking better of the idea.

Half way across the river Kelso pulled up and looked back to see that only two of the hands were with him. He made a sour face, but then with determination he swung around to continue on.

Before Kelso and the other two could take another step, Iron Hair hitched his rifle butt into his shoulder and fired twice. The mounts of both Buck and Clint went down and the riders started flailing in the water.

Kelso pulled up short.

Iron Hair was sitting with his smoking rifle ready to fire again. He was unmoving but waiting. Kelso got the message. His breath came with some difficulty, but he turned around and started back. He reached for Buck's arm and signaled the other ranch hands to help Clint. Following orders Curly moved forward, his rope in his hand, to get the young man out of the river.

Kelso hauled Buck by the arm to the river bank. Curly dallied his rope and backed up pulling Clint's leg free from under his horse. He kept pulling the young cowboy all the way back to shore. When both riders were safely on land, Kelso glanced back at Iron Hair once more. The Indian had his weapon back resting on his thigh again.

Then with Buck and Clint riding double, Kelso led the cowboys back toward the ranch.

* * *

Back at Rancho Lajitas Kelso dismounted, casting a disgruntled glance at the cowboys. Then the foreman handed the reins of his lathered horse to Pepi. With a sigh of resignation, Tom Kelso alone walked up to the solidly built and well maintained hacienda. The other cowboys saw to their horses and waited to see what was going to be next.

At the large heavy wooden front doors, Kelso stopped and waited for a moment before he reached for the metal knocker. He finally knocked on the door with determination.

The door was soon opened by Consuelo, a thin, elderly Mexican housekeeper. She was surprised to see him there.

"Señor Kelso?" Consuelo asked.

The foreman removed his hat.

"Consuelo. Is — ah — Lord Bristol — is he up yet?"

"Si, Señor."

# CHAPTER FIVE

The cool inside of the hacienda was a work of art. Heavy dark wood was accented by alcoves in the adobe walls and colorful paintings of British landscapes and family portraits.

Consuelo was dressed in a white Mexican dress with vividly stitched flowers across the bodice and around the bottom hem of the skirt. She wore leather sandals that shuffled across the tiled floor.

As the pair walked the hallway, a fleeting glance of a beautiful young woman in her very early 20's crossed in front of them. She spoke and backed up. Audrey was the lovely daughter of the owner. She was dressed in a riding skirt and top along with tall boots.

"Mr. Kelso?" she said with surprise.

"Miss Audrey," Kelso answered without his usual friendliness.

"Señor Kelso is here to see your papa."

"Thank you, Consuelo. I'll take him."

Consuelo withdrew as Audrey looped her arm with the foreman's arm.

"What brings you up here this —," she started but Kelso cut her off.

"I have t' see your father. Now!"

Audrey sensed the urgency about Kelso and dropped her playful air.

"This way," she said. "He's having breakfast."

She ushered Kelso into the dining room.

Like the rest of the hacienda, there was such elegance about the house that combined the influences of classic English tapestries and paintings along with some woodwork with heavy Mexican style furniture. Seated at the end of an extended table, behind all the silverware and gold rimmed plates, was Lord Wilford Bristol. He was being served breakfast by a Mexican houseboy.

Lord Bristol, 50, was both a scholarly and distinguished looking gentleman with muttonchops and mustache. He was reading a novel which was beside his plate as Audrey and Kelso entered.

Lord Bristol looked up, first at Audrey, then turned quickly to Kelso.

"Good morning, my dear. Mr. Kelso."

Kelso was nervous. He fidgeted, constantly moving his hat which he held in his hands.

Bristol was now aware that something was amiss. He put his own cup down carefully, dabbed his mouth.

"What is it?"

Kelso glanced over at Audrey, then turned to Lord Bristol.

"It's — Trafalgar, sir."

The alarm, although controlled, did register on Bristol's face.

"Trafalgar? Is he sick — hurt?

Audrey stepped around behind her father and placed a hand on his shoulder. She looked very concerned at Kelso.

"No, sir. He's — all right, 'far as I know."

"What is it, then?"

Kelso took a breath, then spat it out.

"He's been stolen."

Bristol responded with logic not emotion and remained very much in control.

Kelso continued. "We follered th' tracks down to th' Rio."

"Didn't you cross the river? Go after him?"

"Started to. But one of Ortiz's men was there — a Comanch — named Iron Hair. I've seen him b'fore. He was jest sittin' an' waitin'.

He put a bullet in two of our horses. It could have been in two of our hands."

"Ortiz. He's that Mexican General."

"That's what he calls himself. But he's just a damn Comanchero. Ortiz's ol' man and his brothers were all thieves, bandits, and killers. Got themselves killed smugglin' guns."

Bristol stood and crossed to the window looking out on the empty corral.

"You're sure it's Ortiz?"

"I didn't see him, but I know Iron Hair. He wears Otriz's brand."

Lord Bristol took off his house jacket and tossed it in the chair where he had sat.

"Where do we find this — General Ortiz?"

"Cross th' Rio, due South — a day's ride. Lord Bristol, you ain't thinkin' about goin' after them?"

"I think we have little choice. Mr. Kelso, you get the men prepared. I shall draw my own weapons and join you in ten minutes."

Lord Bristol left the room in a hurry but not in a panic.

# CHAPTER SIX

Kelso stood on the porch of the bunkhouse one step behind Lord Bristol and Audrey. Buck Lyle, Curly, Clint, and the other cowboys stood around nervously. Lord Bristol was waiting for a response from the crew.

Finally, it was Buck Lyle, 30's with a couple of day's growth of beard on his face, who spoke.

"Six months wages." He whistled. "But it would be suicide t' ride against Ortiz. I still hope t' get married an' have a place a' my own. Can't do that by bein' dead in Mexico."

Kelso glanced at Lord Bristol to see his reaction. Bristol nodded his head.

"I can appreciate that. How about the rest of you?"

No one spoke. Lord Bristol realized no one wanted to take his offer.

"All right. I will up the price. Five hundred dollars a man. Per day."

Again, there was a long pause during which the cowboys stood shuffling their feet. Clint stepped forward.

"I'll take that."

Buck turned shaking his head.

"I think I'd best get my possibles t'gether. It's 'bout time fer me t' be driftin' on, I 'spect," Buck Lyle said.

Kelso was somewhat alarmed.

"Hold it, Buck. Lord Bristol, can I speak t' you a second?"

Kelso moved inside the bunkhouse door. Bristol was puzzled by these developments, but nodded and followed Kelso inside. Audrey went, too.

After Kelso closed the door, he said, "You're about to lose every hand we got — 'cept Clint and he's young and too full of piss and kerosene to know what he'd be up against."

"What's it going to take? A thousand dollars per man?"

"Not even a thousand dollars will do a man much good if he's toes up, six feet down."

"Are you telling me these men are cowards?"

"No, sir, I ain't. They all ride for the brand — and Buck's a top hand. But these men ain't gunfighters. They're two-dollar-a-week cowpunchers."

"Every one of them carries a gun."

"Yes, sir, an' they're more apt t' get their foot shot off as t' hit a rattlesnake or somethin' else they're aimin' at. They signed on t' wrangle — not t' get killed fightin' Comancheros."

"I thought you told me you didn't think this Ortiz was a real general."

"I did. But I didn't say he was real stupid. Ortiz has almost an army around him. His hacienda is more like a fort than a house. All we'd do would be t' ride in there an' get our heads blowed off."

Audrey stepped forward saying, "Father, Mr. Kelso may be right. Isn't there another way?"

Bristol thought about this for a moment before he said, "Suppose we offer this — bandit — a reward. Do you think he'd return Trafalgar?"

"I doubt it. I hear he's got more than enough gold an' silver t' live a couple of lifetimes."

"Then what does he want?"

"Th' horse. Everyone on the border knows there's no horse like Trafalgar. But these cowboys ain't goin' t' be able t' get him back."

Bristol mulled this over and looked to his daughter before he nodded his head in agreement.

"So, how do we go about it? I cannot leave him there."

Kelso took a deep breath.

"There's a man — . Yeah, he might be able t'."

"Who is he?"

"Name's Maxwell. Clay Maxwell. Used t' be a Texas Ranger. He's retired now. Lives near Del Rio."

"Then by all means, let's get him down here and talk to him."

"Ah — he ain't th' kind a' man who'll come t' anybody. If we want t' talk t' him — we'll have t' do th' goin'."

"Then let's be about just that."

# ABOUT THE AUTHOR

Jack R. Stanley is a native Texan born two blocks inside Texas and raised six blocks inside Arkansas in Texarkana, Arkansas/Texas. He received his B.F.A. from Texas Christian University in Ft. Worth in Radio-TV-Film. As an officer in the U.S. Army serving in Vietnam as a TV-Film Director, he was awarded the Bronze Star. He says when you're in a firefight and you have a camera when everybody else on both side have guns, you get to change your pants a lot.

After his military service he earned both his M.A. and his Ph.D. at the University of Michigan in Ann Arbor in Radio-TV-Film. He also received two of Michigan's most prestigious creative writing awards, The Hopwood Award, one for a one-act play and the second for a novel. His novels are available to Amazon.com in paperback.

Stanley's first academic position was TV Area Head at The University of Texas at Austin's Department of Radio-TV-Film. He later moved to deep south Texas and the Lower Rio Grande Valley for a challenging position with The University of Texas-Pan American. Here he taught Theatre-TV-Film for 30 years in the Department of Communication serving as Department Chair at U.T.P.A. for 11 years. He did take one year out to work for The University of Alaska Anchorage as a visiting professor. Back in Texas, Stanley directed for stage at The University Theatre, produced and directed fifteen student staffed, cast, and crewed feature films, writing most of the original screenplays. A very few of his credits are available on IMDB.com.

Stanley, happily married to his high school sweetheart for over 50 years, now lives in the Texas Panhandle where he writes his fiction and runs his blog, *www.TheFictionWritersNotebook.com*. His e-mail address is. jacks@wrightbridgepress.com

# THANK YOU

Thank you for taking the time to read **13 Steps To Hell**. If you enjoyed it, please consider telling your friends and posting a short review. Word of mouth is an author's best friend and much appreciated. I love to write these stories but it's even better to sell some and know other people take some joy from them, too.

Thank you,

Jack R. Stanley

## TWO FREE E-BOOKS

### [Murder in Muleshoe]
If you were murdered would they try to find the killer or plan him a parade?

### [Guns Along The Rio]Rio
In 1858, two fresh-off-the-ranch 17-year-olds join the Texas Rangers. What could possibly go wrong?

Go To: http://eepurl.com/dKEi_Y

Klondike Justice

Dangerous Camp On The Kenai

The Winds of Skagway

*Screenplays*

6 and 10

The 7<sup>th</sup> Luger

Afternoon Delight

Angel's Revenge

Between Love And Murder

Blood Drive

Death Scene

The Defection of Grigori Dorsky

The Evil Eye

Fatty and Hearst

Gideon: The Horse That Saved Texas

Hell In Paradise

Hollowpoint

Holiday For An Assassin

Horse Thief Hollow

Incident At Lajitas

Love, Lust, & Life

Mom & Apple Pye

Pancho's Pilot

The Prometheus Peril

The Rape of Sarah Quinn

Reservations

River of Tears

Seven Reasons Why

The Thing About Love

www.ingramcontent.com/pod-product-compliance
Lightning Source LLC
Chambersburg PA
CBHW051954170626
46808CB00007B/2613